Cthulhu Fhtagn, Baby!

Cthulhu Fhtagn, Baby!

(and Other Cosmic Insolence)

by

Will Ludwigsen

Printed in the United States of America
Cover art copyright 2006 by Deena Warner.

Published as a trade paperback original
by Lethe Press, 102 Heritage Avenue, Maple Shade, NJ 08052
lethepress@aol.com
LethePress.com

First U.S. edition, 2006

ISBN 1-59021-052-2

Library of Congress Cataloging-in-Publication Data

Ludwigsen, Will.
  Cthulhu fhtagn, baby! (and other cosmic insolence) / by Will
Ludwigsen. -- 1st
U.S. ed.
     p. cm.
  ISBN 1-59021-052-2 (trade pbk.)
  1. Horror tales, American. I. Title.
  PS3612.U35C75 2007
  813'.6--dc22
                          2006038449

Table of Contents

To Norman Amemiya:

You are a freakish abomination to everything the mundane world holds dear. That's the highest compliment I can pay you.

Without you, this book wouldn't exist.

"The Sardonic Enigma"

An Introduction by
Matthew Warner

The chances are that you don't know anything about Will Ludwigsen other than that he has a strange last name (pronounced LUD-wig-zin). So allow me to introduce my friend and collaborator of the past five years.

If I can. You see, Will Ludwigsen and his writing are in some ways an enigma to me, as I believe they are to him. What I do know is that, unlike me, Will is not a self-promoting egoist, which is one reason for his anonymity. Another reason no doubt is that, although he excels at writing, he hasn't yet figured out what kind of writer he is. Just look at some of the magazines he's appeared in— These are tippy-top markets, the flagships of their respective genres, and they're almost impossible to get into. That he's earned the brass ring not once but several times says something about his skill. But because he has refused to allow himself to be pigeonholed into a single area, Will hasn't established a presence in any one of them that's large enough to garner the recognition he deserves. Hopefully, this book—his first—will correct that oversight. It's only because he's written slightly more horror than anything else that this collection is being marketed to horror readers and that its title references a story by the late great horror writer H.P. Lovecraft.

The stories here clearly reflect Will's diversity of interests. Here you have a writer who's experimenting not only with subject matter but with style, point of view, and tone. He's taking chances, often with surprising flashes of originality. (After reading about the beefboxes in "Billy," I guarantee you'll never look at a hamburger the same way again.)

Another thread binding these stories together is the author's sardonic sense of humor. I experienced it firsthand while collaborating with him on "Riders," which is not in this collection but was published in the magazine Tales of the Unanticipated. Thanks to Will, a true horror story about a stalker at my bus stop turned into pastiche about horse breeding.

It's through his humor that we get a sense of Will's mission as a writer, particularly with regard to horror. The stand-up comic in "Exit Laughing" is an avatar of Will's outlook when he states, "I can't fight it, so I do the only thing that's left to me: I mock it. I reduce the horror to something small and manageable by laughing at it. And I make others laugh at it, too."

It reminds me of a recent experience at a science fiction convention in Ohio. At a group dinner, I sat across the table from a stereotypical sci-fi fan: that is, a simian with the hygiene of a vagrant and the social skills of a turnip. He said that when he heard airliners had crashed into the World Trade Center on 9/11, he laughed—an act he re-created with earsplitting shrillness—and cracked a tasteless joke about lost luggage.

I decided I didn't want to spend the night in jail, so I continued chewing my lukewarm egg foo yong. In the awkward silence that followed, however, I realized he wasn't the only person who uses that coping strategy when faced with life's horrors and evils. How many of us have ever made a tasteless joke about the O.J. Simpson murders or quadriplegic amputees? We laugh, expelling the psychological steam of revulsion, so we don't blow apart. Will's stories perform that same function by reducing life's grotesqueries to the level of absurdity, whether he's dealing with homelessness, deformity, or necrophilia. Anyone who can do that, even for a little while, deserves our thanks.

That being said, Will's use of humor, while being his greatest strength as a writer, is also his greatest liability. One man's humor is another man's offense, just as I was offended by the clueless dork at the science fiction convention. If you find yourself in the latter category, I ask you to just shrug and turn to the next story. With a collection so varied, you're bound to find something pleasing.

I think the best stories in this collection are the ones that leaven the humor with a healthy dose of other qualities. Will has admitted to me that he can use humor to hide from deeper emotions. This is reflected in those stories that rely solely on humor; while they're certainly original and expertly crafted, they run the risk of being soulless. Conversely, those stories that mix humor with love and sympathy contain characters who are real people and themes with direct bearing on our lives. I'm thinking of "Nessmas," "Billy," "And Justice for Doll," and "Bingo." These four stories in particular are quite moving and worthy of second reads.

I've spent most of my space here telling you about Will's writing and not much about him as a person. The biographical details are that he's in his early thirties, has been married twice, and has no vices other than a taste for sugary drinks. He lives in Ohio but is destined to move to the Shenandoah Valley to be near his friend Matthew Warner. He wears eyeglasses and an immaculately groomed goatee. He has all his hair. To support his fiction habit, he works part-time as a technical writer for the U.S. Census Bureau, a job that requires him to visit Washington, DC, once per month. I suspect he wouldn't do that if DC didn't contain its monuments and museums, which he likes to visit for some strange reason. Will excels at political commentary and at writing instruction, which you can sample through his blog at will-ludwigsen.com and his Horror World column at horrorworld.org.

Now, without further ado, I invite you to take a seat here by the stage. As you listen, you might try our home brews—store clerk's urine and sour milk—while sampling a tasty beefbox. Try not to glance at the playbill with the squid-faced gentleman on the cover; you might go insane.

Oh, and pardon the entrails.

Matthew Warner
Staunton, Virginia
November 1, 2006

Foreword

Writers, like comedians, require a shtick. Denis Leary is the "high-strung-cigarette-smoking" guy. Dennis Miller is the "arcane-reference-out-of-nowhere" guy. Gallagher is the "crushing-watermelons-with-a-sledgehammer" guy.

Writers call it something pretentious like a "voice" or a "thematic preoccupation," but it boils down to a shtick: something that makes a writer easily identifiable to his or her fans. Heinlein is the "square-jawed-conservatives-with-a-strange-need-to-be-naked" guy. Lovecraft is the "sinister-seafood-too-advanced-to-even-notice-us" guy. And somehow I've become the "strange-stories-that-make-you-laugh-but-then-also-disquiet-you" guy.

I didn't set out to do that, but I come by it honestly. John Ruskin wrote, "Tell me what you like and I'll tell you what you are," and by that standard, my family and I are people who fight evil by laughing at it. It was, indeed, our only weapon during our most terrible times. Too classy to appear on *Cops*, we chose to become the Addams Family instead.

My sister scratched on my window after *Salem's Lot* appeared on television and now educates people about infectious disease (probably because she just thinks it is cool). My mother clutched her chest when the whales swam across the IMAX screen during *Fantasia 2000* and yelled, "Holy shit!" in the company of a hundred blushing Catholic schoolchildren. Our knickknacks include organ models and severed deer heads. We have never had a meal during which tuberculosis, ebola, gangrene, or diarrhea have not come up as topics of conversation or, alas, demonstration.

We're dark. Not sad-sack-Goth dark, but cheery-demented dark. We're black-cloaked optimists laughing on the way to our execution, hoping that wit and savoir-faire count for something in the face of evil.

Maybe Karen has scratched your window and made you a member of our family, too.

Those of us who love snickering in the darkness understand a fundamental truth missed by all the grinning pollyannas: anyone who thinks that this is the best of all possible worlds is the bleakest of pessimists, and only those who understand that we are here to cultivate our fallen Garden of Eden with our most imaginative and flamboyant lies know true optimism.

Oscar Wilde wrote that "the real tragedies of life occur in such an inartistic manner that they hurt us by their crude violence, their absolute incoherence, their absurd want of meaning, their entire lack of style." A horror writer fixes that by making better horrors: ones with coherence and meaning and style. We fight evil by naming it, by knowing it, by laughing at it until it shrinks.

These are silly little stories, hardly worth the time to read them. Yet they still have more style than the brutish horrors that truly surround us. We laugh because our imagination always trumps the real world— always.

Have a seat at the table, will you?

Anomie

You're working through school and have come to believe that the smocks they give you at the Coastal Mart convenience store have the words "Please fuck with me" written on them in dye visible only to rats and bums. It's the only explanation for the abuse you get while peddling gas, cigarettes, and issues of "Juggs" magazine.

Daily, paragons of bumness (Bumhood? Bumnity?) stagger into the store. You can never tell if they're drunk, mentally ill, or just working some unknowable agenda. They're drawn to your store like possums to a cow carcass.

You put a good spin on it and think of them as subjects for your senior thesis. All you need is a theme. You have the title: "Bums in the Mist."

Your touchstone subject, ready for immortality in your paper, lives behind the store under a scrap of sheet metal. If he were ten, he'd call it a fort. At forty, he calls it a home. Every day, he shambles in, careening from the chips to the candy to the coolers. He pulls a beer from the rack and cuddles it against his chest as he returns to the counter.

You're mandated by the corporate office to say, "Good afternoon, sir. Welcome to Coastal. Would you like anything else with your beer?"

He is mandated by the vagrant corporate office to say, "Gimme a lottery ticket."

You peel one off the reel underneath the counter and slide it across to him. He scoops a fistful of change out of his pocket and slams it on the counter. A coin or two rolls off onto the floor but he doesn't go after them. He can beg for more.

You count it and sweep it into the drawer while he leaves to enjoy his beer in the comfort of his fort/home.

One day, he returns with the bottle after being outside for ten minutes and sets it on the counter.

"It's warm," he says.

You feel the bottle and sure enough, he's right. A minute ago, it was ice cold. Could it have warmed up that fast? After all, it is Florida and hence as hot as the surface of the sun outside, but maybe it really was warm to begin with. It would suck to panhandle all day so you can wet your throat, but then your beer turns out to be warm.

"I'd like to get another one," he says.

Corporate policy says the customer is always right, and so you shrug and point back to the cooler. He fetches himself another and then leaves the store wearing a strange grin.

You look down at the opened bottle. It's mostly full but the cap is gone. You stoop closer and realize when you take a whiff that it's full of urine.

It's the oldest trick in the bum handbook: he buys a beer, guzzles it down behind the store, and then pisses in the empty bottle so he can take it back and get another one. It's a two-for-one deal and all it requires is that the bum reserve some of the urine he usually splashes on the side of the store.

Pretty sneaky.

But he's met his match in you, a psychology major. Not three months ago you discussed in class the concept of anomie, where social mores erode with every passing generation. In the violent poker game of society, Charles Manson's straight is no match for David Koresh's flush, and poor Lizzie Borden (with her mere forty whacks) doesn't even have the chips to ante up. What will be the apex of this evolution? What will our progeny watch on Saturday morning television that hardened police officers can't stomach today? In a flash of genius, you've got the theme for your thesis. You scrawl it on a scrap of register tape and shove it in your pocket.

Here's what you do.

Weeks later, he comes back in again (he waits, hoping you'll forget what happened). You smile and toe the company line. He buys his beer and you take his coins. He leaves the store, only to return a few minutes later with a warm beer.

He's right where you want him.

"Can I have another one, please? This one's warm."

This time, you play it up. "Warm? How can that be? We serve nothing but the highest quality beer here at Coastal!"

With a look of concern you lift the bottle.

"Well, you're right!" you say. "It is warm. I wonder if the beer is still good."

And then you tip the bottle up to your lips and take a big mouthful. It's warm and salty in your mouth and it's all you can do to stop yourself from gagging. You twist your face into an approximation of a smile. You nod, sloshing it around in your mouth like a fine wine, remembering that Professor Schwassman told you in biology class that urine is sterile.

The bum's eyes bulge like a squid's. His legs twitch while he tries to decide if he wants to run.

You keep nodding. Slosh, slosh. *Urine is sterile. Urine is sterile.*

The bum retreats in horror. Something deep in his soul tries to goad him into telling you the truth, but his schizophrenia stomps it down again. He steps back from the counter.

Not far enough.

You stop and make a face of revulsion and disgust. He opens his mouth to exclaim, and it is right then that you release your mouthful in a spray all over him.

"I am so sorry!" you say, donning that gentle face you wear for clients at the clinic. "I just couldn't get it down. Can I get you some paper towels?"

The man sprints from the store, slipping outside on a patch of oil and then scuttling like a crab through the parking lot.

Yeah, you think to yourself. I've got your anomie right here. I'll call your bluff and raise you.

You scrawl another note in your textbook and keep studying.

And Justice for Doll

I think my grandchildren enjoy my company solely because I am too slow to get away. While their parents escape to work all summer, I am captive audience for a parade of magic shows, puppet shows, song recitals, recorder concerts, and art gallery expositions that my son's kids contrive to entertain themselves between school years.

Of course, few things entertain three intelligent and independent kids more than arguing over whose turn it is to vacuum or who gets the last Coke or who left the moldy towel in the tub. I've arbitrated more disputes in my son's living room than I did over thirty years both before and behind the bench.

Don't get me wrong: I love my son's children. Holly, fourteen, loves me to take her to the modern art museum, the only place her disdainful Dorothy Parker gaze melts into awe. Eric, thirteen, tinkers with electronics and computers; he wrote a program so we could track the player statistics for the Giants together. But Jessica, eight, stands out to me most of all.

Maybe there's something special about the youngest, the one who can't reach the cabinets or be a part of every conversation. Maybe it's her earnestness while orchestrating Christmas morning or trying to teach the cats to read. Maybe I'm just endeared to her ambition to be a lawyer when she grows up, like her grandfather.

Like any youngest child, Jessica has inherited a legion of dolls and stuffed animals in various stages of hand-me-down decay. They appear throughout the house, keeping Jessica's seat warm at the dinner table and waiting by the mailbox for the latest issue of *Ranger Rick*. I've even crushed a few sitting in my favorite chair in the living room.

This summer, they organized as a democratic body to establish Babytown, a community within my son's house where toys would not be discriminated against on a basis of age, condition, or third world country of manufacture.

The pun between Babytown and Jonestown was inadvertent but apt: this utopia also followed a single charismatic leader. Lavinia, the alpha doll chosen to go to restaurants and the Fourth of July fireworks, won a landslide victory in the mayoral race. The masking tape patch over the crack in her plastic skull probably didn't help during the debates, but it did motivate enough of a sympathy vote to vault her into power.

Lavinia and the other Babytown dignitaries weren't above a little politicking, even on the morning of their revolution. They took the time to introduce themselves in a variety of heavily accented voices that Jessica imitated from television. The list seemed endless, at least measured by how long it took me to read the Metro section while Jessica trooped them past. I met in turn the hospital administrator (an Ewok with a Scottish brogue), the school superintendent (a Cabbage Patch doll with Martha Stewart's calm monotone), the theater proprietor (a Kermit with a nasal twang I couldn't place), and a dozen others.

"And this," said Jessica, holding up the last, "is the chief of police." My son's first teddy bear, mouth agape in surprise to see the millennium, wore a tin badge pinned to his chest.

I looked up from my paper. "Chief of police?"

She held him up to her face and drawled on his behalf, "Howdy, stranger. Welcome to town." She extended his paw.

I shook it. "Is there crime in Babytown?"

Jessica shrugged. "Not yet. But you never know."

"Is there a crime lab? A forensics team?" I imagined dolls clad in white coats considering crayon marks and filling plaster casts of hind paw impressions.

"No, silly."

"What about a legal system? What protects the rights of the accused?"

Jessica narrowed her eyes at me like she often did when I mentioned ancient concepts like full service gas stations. "They're just *babies*, Grandpa. They don't do bad things."

"Is that so? You'd better check with your mother about that." I lifted my paper again. I'd heard other misguided government officials claim low crime rates didn't require well-funded courts.

Jessica, Lavinia, and the people of Babytown conducted their daily business and spread through every room like invading hordes. Their town hall was the living room, and I tried to tune out the whispering and giggling between Jessica and her minions as they discussed the pressing issues of their fledgling democracy.

They'd just passed a resolution condemning green beans when someone got hungry enough to take a break. Jessica turned to me and said, "I'm going to get popsicles for the council. Do you want one?"

"No thanks."

I heard the footstool scrape across the kitchen floor and the freezer door open. I was folding the comics page into a square to do the crossword when her ear-withering scream sent my heart into arrhythmia.

I rushed to the kitchen, afraid Jessica's head had cracked like Lavinia's against the tile, but she stood pointing into the freezer.

There, nestled in the clumps of snow and encased in a block of ice, was Sun N' Fun Barbie.

"W-who did that, Grandpa?"

I pulled Barbie from her icy tomb and set her in the sink to thaw. "I don't know. Looks like a case for the Babytown police."

It wasn't long before the authorities discovered Barbie was only the first victim of a grim toyland Helter Skelter. Innocent citizens found dolls and stuffed animals displayed in grisly poses: a plush cat crushed under the couch leg, a baby doll hanging from the ceiling fan chain, a Weeble wobbling at the bottom of the toilet, and others too hideous to describe.

The chief of police announced during one of Jessica's frequent news conferences that he would focus his scrutiny on Eric, known for taking sick glee in teasing his little sister and previously implicated in the Great Bacon Grease Frosting Debacle and the Great You-Were-Adopted Hoax.

Eric, no fool, decided to make a hasty escape. A game of Risk tucked under his arm, he waved on his way to the door.

"I'm going over to Mark's for the afternoon, Grandpa."

"That's fine. Be back by four."

Jessica's olive face flushed in a burgundy rage. "No, you're not!" She leaped, knocking the game from Eric's grasp in a shower of plastic armies.

"Hey!" He shoved her back and ran outside to his bicycle.

"Okay, now." I rose from my chair.

Jessica grabbed an angry stuffed animal posse and chased Eric into the yard, shrieking "Murderer!"

By the time I got out there, she was pounding her fists against his stomach, her pigtails whipping around like a nest of angry asps. "You killed them, you monster!"

The mailman halted at the end of the driveway, clutching my son's bills to his chest.

"Just a little childhood conflict," I said, forcing a laugh.

I pushed the kids apart and tugged them inside by their elbows. "Let's pretend we're not a family of sociopaths, shall we?"

Eric and Jessica both nodded curtly to the mailman.

After the screen door clattered shut behind us, Jessica renewed her assault. "Murderer! He killed my baby dolls!"

"Yeah?" Eric grinned. "Prove it."

"I don't have to. Grandpa knows you did it."

I tried to climb to neutral ground. "I didn't see anything."

"Neither did she."

"The babies were in every room. They all saw it. They're witnesses!" An idea crackled through Jessica's brain and glowed behind her eyes. She jabbed a finger at Eric in true Banquo fashion and cried, "You are under arrest!"

"For what?"

"For murder. First degree murder."

"Where are you going to prove it, you twisted little gnome?"

"In Babytown court with Grandpa as judge."

"Oh, no," I said, holding up my hands. "I have to recuse myself for conflict of interest. I'm related to both the defendant and the prosecution."

"So you're saying you love one of us more than the other?" asked Jessica.

"What? No, of course not."

"Doesn't that make you the most impartial judge around? Aren't you more fair because you love both of us the same?"

Had the trial already begun? If I didn't think fast, she'd have me back on the bench. "Well, maybe. But I retired as a defense attorney, not a judge."

"Fine," said my grandson. "You're hired."

"Wait a minute——"

"Holly!" Jessica called her sister with a shrill voice capable of penetrating solid lead.

Holly leaned out from her bedroom, dance music throbbing behind her. "What is it?"

"We need you to be a judge."

"What are you talking about?"

"I'm putting Eric in jail for killing my babies."

"I'm doing my nails."

"All you have to do is listen." Jessica put her hands on her hips.

"No. Get somebody else to play along."

"Well, I guess we could have one of my friends come over, but that'd take a long time."

"Oprah is on at four."

"If we had a judge we might be done by then."

The music stopped. Holly shuffled into the living room with tufts of cotton between her drying toenails. "Whatever. Let's get on with it."

Jessica gathered a courtroom crowd of Babytown citizens and pointed every pair of eyes toward the couch where Eric and I sat. Holly shoved the recliner into position so she could take the bench.

"All rise!" cried Jessica. "The Babytown criminal court is now in session, with the Honorable Judge Holly Driscoll presiding."

Eric and I rose. Holly waved to us to sit down and opened her sketch pad. She drew excellent portraits in pencil, especially when inspired by boredom.

Her Honor sighed. "What's first?"

"Opening arguments," I said.

Jessica strode to the front of the living room.

"Murder." She shook her head. "Murder isn't supposed to happen in Babytown. It's a happy place, where we make special nametags for everyone at Thanksgiving and where we help Mommy with the laundry even when everyone else is too busy. Then Eric—always an enemy of the babies and Babytown—attacked us for no reason. I intend to prove to the court that Eric planned these crimes and isn't sorry he did them."

She was better than many prosecutors I remember.

"Grandpa?"

I cleared my throat. "Your Honor, I believe you will find the prosecution's case is circumstantial, relying on my client's previous crimes to convict."

"That's it?" Eric whispered.

"Short and simple, son. Judges like that."

The prosecution called her first witness, the mayor.

Lavinia's plastic hand rested on the *Illustrated Bible for Children* while an Admiral Ackbar action figure swore her in. "Do you swear to tell the truth, the whole truth, and nothing but the truth?"

"I do," said Lavinia in a baby voice emanating from the prosecution's pursed lips.

"Oh, boy," said Eric. "Here we go."

I nudged him with my elbow.

"Mayor Lavinia," said Jessica with drama observed from watching *Law and Order* with her mother. "Please tell us what you saw earlier today."

The mayor quivered. "I saw..."

"It's okay, Lavinia," soothed Jessica. "We'll protect you here."

"Come on." Eric groaned. "This is going to take a hundred years."

The prosecution stuck out her tongue at my client.

Lavinia continued. "I was in the back bedroom and I saw Eric wrapping the chain of the ceiling fan around Baby Helen's neck. She swung there for a second before she fell to the ground."

"And what did the bad, bad defendant do at this point?"

"Objection!" I cried. "Leading the witness."

"Sustained."

Jessica scowled. "What did Eric do, Lavinia?"

"He laughed."

"He laughed. No further questions."

I didn't have much for cross. "Was anyone else in the room at the time?"

"No. Only Eric, the murderer." Jessica turned Lavinia's head to face Eric with defiance.

"Are you certain? Not Jessica?"

"No. Just me and that evil boy."

"No further questions."

Brown Bear, more beige than brown when he was once my client's property, took the stand.

"Could you describe to the court what you saw, Brown Bear?"

"Yes," said Brown Bear. "I—"

My client cut him off. "For God's sake, she's making them talk. She's just using different voices!"

Judge Holly looked up from her pencil sketch of my client. "One more outburst and you'll be held in contempt."

"Is he even allowed to testify against me? He was my bear when I was little. Isn't that a conflict of interest or something?"

"Sorry, son," I said. "We're in Babytown jurisdiction now."

Eric kicked the coffee table.

The prosecution patted Brown Bear's paw. "Please continue."

"I watched Eric as he took down one of Daddy's large beer glasses—
"

"—strictly forbidden to every kid in this house, correct?" Jessica interrupted herself.

"Yes," said Brown Bear. "But it was the only one tall enough to contain Barbie. So I saw him fill it with water from the sink, drop Barbie in it, and put the glass in the freezer behind the orange Popsicles."

"To hide her long enough to freeze."

"Yes." Brown Bear's voice cracked with emotion.

"Thank you."

Something seemed wrong to me. "How could you have seen Eric place Barbie in the beer glass when Jessica was out here conducting Babytown meetings?"

"Because Jessica left me on the counter to guard the Babytown food supply when she came in for breakfast."

The bear had me. "No further questions."

More witnesses offered further damning testimony. Elmo affirmed he'd watched Eric position Chairman Meow's head under the left forward couch leg in the den. Robot educator 2-XL droned that he observed my client shove Gumby into the mailbox with the obvious intent of melting him into a green goo in the summer heat.

Each new witness confirmed the prosecution's case, and the outcome was almost certain: Eric would be found guilty. I requested a recess from the court to consult with my client in the kitchen.

"Grandpa, she's winning!" Eric reached into the refrigerator for a Sprite. "Dad said you used to get criminals off all the time."

I forced myself to smile. "I didn't get criminals 'off.' I protected their rights from an overzealous criminal justice system that wanted them to go to jail because they were black or poor. Your dad listens to Rush Limbaugh too much."

"Then why are you letting an eight-year-old girl win?"

That's a hard question to ask a grandfather, especially one with a career of a thousand successful defense cases.

"We're not letting her win. We're letting her *think* she's winning. The trick of defense is to let the prosecution weave a quilt of facts and assumptions. Then we yank a thread and unravel it. The more the prosecution says, the more we have to work with."

Eric nodded.

"Now, in case it comes to it, I need to know if you'd be willing to enter a plea." I shivered at the thought of Eric in the Babytown tombs, but I had to cover all the bases.

"Are you asking if I did it?"

I held up my hand. "You never ask that. I just want to know if you'd be willing to negotiate with the prosecution for a lighter sentence."

I could see in Eric's eyes an endless stream of makeovers delivered by the barbarous Babytown penal system.

"No. I'll take my chances."

I put my hand on the boy's shoulder. "It shouldn't come to that."

"If you say so, Grandpa." Eric gulped his soda.

We returned to the courtroom.

"Any further evidence from the prosecution?" Holly nudged Jessica with her foot.

"Nope. The prosecution rests."

"Grandpa?"

I rose and clasped my hands behind my back. Old habits die hard. "Your honor, the defense recalls Brown Bear to the stand."

The front door swung open just as Jessica ran to get him, and my daughter-in-law Julie staggered inside balancing her briefcase and several grocery bags on her knees and arms.

"Hey! You demons want to help me with these?"

The court declared another recess as Eric and Holly donned shoes and trudged outside to fetch the groceries. Jessica scrambled outside barefoot.

"What are you doing standing by the door, Howard? The kids weren't giving you a hard time, were they?" Julie shuffled into the kitchen.

"Oh, no," I said absently, considering my cross-examination and watching Jessica hopping on the hot driveway with a single plastic bag in her hands. What a firebrand she is, I thought. Serious and indignant and ready to right wrongs and serve justice.

Grandfathers—and keep this big secret to yourself—don't always compete to their full abilities. Sometimes we've been known to take a dive. We don't see the move that puts a child's king into checkmate. We don't block all angles in Connect Four. We forget to demand rent when a piece lands on Boardwalk. Something happens to a grandparent that diminishes the need to win, even in an old prize fighter like me.

I'd been known to throw a fight to make Jessica happy. Like any girl with attorney blood surging through her veins, she loved to win. She beamed and walked taller for an hour after. When she won, I won.

I wouldn't need to throw this one for her. She'd pleaded a persuasive case. She'd gathered strong testimony against a client who we all assumed was guilty.

Assumed. Was my granddaughter railroading my client?

I'm a grandfather. I wanted Jessica to win. But I'm also a defense attorney, and she was sandbagging my client with circumstantial and hearsay evidence in a prejudicial venue. Eric's civil rights were in jeopardy, and—guilty as he probably was—he deserved the same vigorous defense guaranteed by the Constitution of the United States.

The kids stormed inside one after the other, fumbling with bags. My client lugged the milk jugs and twelve packs of soda.

This wasn't Chutes and Ladders anymore. I left the bench to defend clients from slick-haired, shiny-suited prosecutors with political ambitions; I couldn't raise my granddaughter to become one.

Once the kids helped put away the groceries, the prosecution retrieved Brown Bear to take the stand. Admiral Ackbar swore him in again.

I started off slowly. "Brown Bear, of what material is your eye constructed?"

"Plastic?" The bear seemed confused.

"Your honor, I'd like to introduce into evidence *The New York Public Library Science Desk Reference*." I pulled the book from the bottom shelf.

Jessica grabbed for it. "That's Daddy's book."

I held it out of her reach. "He won't mind if we borrow it. I direct the court's attention to page 168, describing the function of the eye. To summarize briefly, a lens focuses light in the eye which is then converted to nerve impulses by the retina."

"Objection!"

We all turned. "For?" Holly prompted.

Jessica squirmed in her seat. "Being sneaky."

"Overruled."

I returned to the witness. "Brown Bear, is the plastic of your eyes photoreceptive?"

Brown Bear seemed off balance, like many a perjured witness. "Photo what?"

"Photoreceptive. The retina is photoreceptive, with rods and cones absorbing light. How do your eyes do that?"

"They don't."

"If your eyes cannot perceive light, how could you have seen the defendant wrap the chain leading to the ceiling fan around the victim's throat?"

The bear had no answer.

"Is it not true, Brown Bear," said I, whirling to point at him dramatically, "that you are completely blind?"

The bear stuttered nonsense syllables.

In quick succession, I called each witness in turn and asked pointed questions. Are you manufactured of plastic? Are you too short to see my client? Is it not then impossible that you observed my client committing the crime?

The prosecution had no rebuttal.

I always save the best witness for last. "Your Honor, the defense calls Mayor Lavinia to the stand."

Jessica folded her arms.

"The prosecution will produce the witness or be found in contempt," said Holly.

The prosecution stomped to her room, grabbed Lavinia, and set her on the stand.

I cleared my throat. "Honorable mayor, can you describe the circumstances under which you received—how can I put this delicately—your grievous injury?"

"Unfair!" cried the prosecution.

"May it please the court that this line of questioning speaks toward witness credibility."

Judge Holly nodded. "I'll allow it."

The mayor replied through Jessica's clenched teeth, "One night when Mommy washed me two years ago, I hit my head in the washing machine."

"And you now wear a protective patch of masking tape?"

"Yes."

"Could you please remove the tape to show the court exactly what your head contains?"

The scowling prosecution peeled back the patch to reveal the dark cavity in the mayor's plastic brain case.

"May the court observe the witness's empty head."

"So noted."

"You claim before the court that you recall seeing the defendant at the crime scene. Do you stand by your statement?"

"Yes."

"If so, where do you store those memories without a brain? Is it not possible that any brains you had drained into the washing machine as you banged and spun into unconsciousness that fateful day?"

The mayor stammered.

"No further questions."

Jessica fumed and had no questions for redirect.

"The defense rests."

Holly checked the VCR clock. "Is that it?"

"Closing arguments! Closing arguments!" Jessica cried.

"*Oprah* is on in three minutes. Haven't you said enough?"

"Grandpa!"

"It's Holly's courtroom."

"I've got enough information to make my judgment."

Her Honor retired to the kitchen to pour herself an iced tea and deliberate over the case. Eric and I tried to avoid Jessica's glare.

"You know you did it."

Eric leaned back. "Did what?"

"Killed those babies. I'm writing about this in the Christmas newsletter so nobody will buy you presents this year."

Yellow journalism, too. She learned fast.

"Maybe they all tried to kill themselves to avoid a life in your totalitarian state."

"Shut up."

"No, you shut up."

Holly returned. "Both of you shut up."

As she settled into the recliner, we rose halfway and sat again. "After due deliberation, this court finds the defendant Eric Charles Driscoll not guilty of murder in the first degree and orders him released." She tapped the coffee table with her glass. "Court adjourned."

"I hate you all!" The prosecution ran crying to the bathroom and locked herself inside. Come to think of it, that might be what I did when I lost my first case, too.

I grasped Eric's arm on his way outside and said, "Next time might not go as well, Capone. Don't push your luck. Follow my meaning?"

"Sure, Grandpa."

Holly turned on the television and I walked back to the hallway bathroom. Jessica wailed behind the door.

"Sweetie, you can't win every case. I didn't win every one, even." Her crying grew louder. Had I ruined her love for arguing the law? Had I shattered her innocent zeal for justice?

"You can't just line up witnesses to say whatever you want. Even criminals have rights."

"Go away!"

I pressed my hands against the door. My attorney blood diluted with the grandfatherly kind, and I whispered, "There's always the civil case."

The sobbing stopped.

Nessmas

Ian awakened from a deep slumber with a jab from his wife's elbow to his side.

"Listen!" Marian rasped in the darkness. "Do you hear it?"

Dazed and blinking, Ian strained to listen. Outside the window above the bed, the dark water of the loch slapped against the new dock. A car whooshed by too fast for these narrow roads. A gentle breeze washed through the trees and rustled the leaves beneath them. An owl hooted somewhere far away.

"I don't hear a damned thing," he said, annoyed. "Go back to sleep and stop reading those mystery stories before you—"

A long, slow moan interrupted him by deeply resonating through the windows and vibrating the shafts of his bones. It persisted for several seconds before fading away.

"You see?" she cried. "There it is again! It's coming from the shore."

Ian rolled over to face his wife. "It's just a fog horn."

"What if it isn't?" she asked. "What if someone's in trouble?"

"Serves them right for going out on the loch this time of night."

"Ian! That's horrible. What if it's a wounded animal?"

Ian pulled the wool blanket up around his neck. "Well, we're not taking it in. It's bad enough we've got your brother's bottomless stomach to fill without some animal joining him at the trough."

"Please go see what it is. I won't be able to sleep if I don't know." Marian nudged him.

"It's a log rubbing against old man Clendaniel's seawall. Now you know. Go to sleep."

Again the deep moan rolled through the darkness against the house.

"There it is again! I think it's close. Go see what it is!"

"I'm tired. Send your brother. He's been lounging all day."

"Malcolm's been too sick. He can't go check it out by himself."

"Sick. Yeah, I guess that's a word for it."

They were quiet for several minutes and Ian was just fading back to sleep again when his wife said, "Maybe something is damaging the new dock. Maybe that's the sound of the boards creaking under some heavy weight."

Ian opened one eye. "I doubt it."

"You never know. We haven't had a chance to reinforce it yet." She folded her arms.

"Ah, for the love of God!" Ian sat up and swung his legs out of bed. "I guess I'll go see what it is." He slid his feet into his shoes beside the bed and rose with dramatic groans and murmured epithets. He pulled his coat from a hook behind the door and pulled it on over his pajamas.

"Do be careful!"

Ian looked at his wife and smiled. "I'll try."

Just as he turned to open the bedroom door, she said, "Take Malcolm with you."

"I'm sure he'll come in handy," he muttered to himself as he stepped into the dark hallway. Stumbling through the shadows, he made his way to the living room couch and the lumpy form upon it.

He kicked the leg of the couch. "Wake up, freeloader. We've got work to do."

Malcolm tensed. In a voice garbled by drowsiness, he mumbled, "Isn't it a little early?"

"Yeah," said Ian, yanking open the back door. "It's before noon. Come join me in the backyard at your nearest convenience, your majesty."

He let the door slam behind him and strode into the thick backyard grass near the edge of the loch. Shimmering patches of moonlight shone in the choppy water, and trees swayed back and forth against the sky. Cool air seeped under his coat and chilled his skin.

The door squeaked open and then clattered shut behind him.

"Ooh, it's cold!" Malcolm rubbed his hands on his arms for warmth.

In the corner of the lot a few yards from the dock, Ian saw a dark form lurking in the grass. He squinted and took three steps forward to see it more clearly.

"What the hell is that?" asked Malcolm.

"Quiet down or you'll wake the neighbors! Some of them work." Ian bent lower and walked slowly toward the long, grayish-green lump in the grass. It was easily seventy feet long and six high. It tapered at both ends, coming to a point at one and a rounded bulb at the other. The stench of rotting fish hung in the air.

"No," said Ian quietly as he quickened his approach. "It had better not be… "

He stopped right before a wet, slimy, diamond-shaped flipper wedged into the grass and mud. He stepped beyond it carefully and rushed up to the form.

It was an enormous creature, with a slick, greenish hide glinting in the light from the moon and house lights. Patches of gray fungus mottled its skin, and some were red and raw. As he stood in stunned amazement, the thing's sides expanded and contracted shallowly, and warm mist billowed from its head.

Ian ran toward the head and found a pair of round, glassy eyes fighting a losing battle to remain uncovered by scaly eyelids. The creature's nostrils flared irregularly when a breath managed to find its way in and out of them.

"Jesus Christ!" cried Malcolm behind him. "Do you realize what that is?"

Ian lifted an eyelid, and the orb beneath it was clouded and gray.

"Get a plunger," he said.

Malcolm tried again. "Do you know—"

"I don't care," said Ian impatiently, tensely. "Get a plunger. Now."

Malcolm ran for the house while Ian hurried to the far side of the creature. He pressed his ear against its side and heard throbbing organs struggling for life beneath the cold surface. Something squished deep within, slowing its rhythm with every beat.

Ian pressed his hand against the side lightly at first, and then pushed hard. The flesh was soft beneath the skin and gave beneath his pressure like a bruised tomato.

The door opened and slammed shut. He heard Marian and Malcolm making their way through the yard.

"I'm on the other side," he said as loud as he dared. "And keep your voices down. I don't want to wake the neighbors." He glanced nervously behind him at Clendaniel's rock wall.

Marian came around the front and handed her husband a plunger. "What are we going to do? Can we save it? I'm going to call someone."

"No!" said Ian, slamming the plunger against the side of the creature to make it stick. "We're not calling anybody. Tell the moron to prop open its mouth."

"Oh, no," she said, running back around the creature to the other side. Ian pushed and pulled the plunger rhythmically, and the creature's side moved with it back and forth.

"It's open," cried Malcolm from the front. "It's got big teeth."

Ian kept up his efforts. The sturdy body made rough work, but he kept at it. "Wipe away anything that comes out of the mouth or nose," he commanded.

"There are globs of green jelly stuff coming out."

"Wipe them away!"

"With what?" asked Malcolm.

"Your hand, damn it," Ian snarled. "We've got to keep its airways clear!" He was panting and sweating now.

Malcolm tentatively reached toward the head but pulled his hand away at the last second.

"For God's sake, Malcolm," said Marian as she knelt by the head. She scooped away a large mass of slippery, gelatinous fluid and shook it from her hand to the ground. Water bubbled from its nostrils and oozed down its face.

Ian kept pumping the plunger against its side. "I'm getting tired!"

"Go help him." Marian pointed at Ian. Malcolm turned to help just as one final, titanic groan escaped the creature's mouth and a spray of water and mucous splattered against him. Suddenly, it was very still and its eyes were frozen in surprise.

Ian stopped and collapsed into the grass beside the creature, leaving the plunger's handle to wriggle up and down like the finger of a disappointed parent.

"Is that it?" cried Marian. "Keep trying! It's not dead yet! It's just…"

Ian panted and mopped his brow with his sleeve. He opened his mouth to speak, but then closed it again as if nothing would come out that he wanted to say.

"Shouldn't we call a doctor or a veterinarian or a policeman?"

Ian struggled to his feet. "What could they do? The same thing we did - nothing." Wiping his hands against his pants, he walked toward his wife. He hugged her close to him and they settled down to sit on the damp grass. She sobbed against his coat collar, and he rocked her back and forth.

Beside the creature, Malcolm began to pace with his hands clasped behind his back. He nodded to himself and seemed to be muttering.

They mourned in their own ways in the moonlight for close to half an hour: Ian and Marian held each other while Malcolm considered a plan. When his sister's sobs had subsided, Malcolm turned to face them both. "Do you remember, Marian, when Mum used to say that every time the Lord closed a door, He opened a window?"

She nodded, sniffling. Ian eyed him suspiciously.

"Now this here looks like a big ugly door has slammed in our face, doesn't it? A natural wonder that has brought prosperity to our lives has died. Poor Nessie has breathed her last."

Marian began to sob again.

Ian squinted at Malcolm. "Whenever you start talking so poetically, boy, is when I know the shit is coming out."

Malcolm scowled but continued. "This is a big door, but I think it's also a window. We have right before us the evidence we've sought all our lives that something lives in this loch. We're the only people on Earth who know exactly what Nessie is and what she looks like. This is our big chance to know the truth about Nessie, and to share that truth with the world."

"Share? That's not like you, Malcolm."

Malcolm smiled. "Well, the truth certainly isn't free. But we've got it right here - the evidence the whole world has been waiting to see that there are still wonders of the world, and that they're right here in Loch Ness!"

Ian rested his head in his hands and barked out a brief, bitter laugh. "This is amazing. Poor Nessie's body is barely cold and you're already plotting a way to make a quick buck from it? Jesus, Malcolm, if you spent this much energy and thought on real work, you'd be a wealthy man."

"I think about work all the time. It consumes me. The difference between us is that you think the only way to do things is to grimly push and push until they get done, while I try to do things with a little flair and strategy. Your way is fine in some cases. People like you pushed huge stones to make the pyramids—but people like me designed them. That's the difference, Ian. To you, everything in life is a new problem to endure or overcome with brute force. To me, it's an opportunity."

Ian raised his eyebrows. "Really? That brute force is keeping a roof over your head, isn't it?"

Malcolm ignored him. "Look at this situation. To you, this is a big problem. 'Boo, hoo. Nessie's dead.' 'Boo hoo, I've got twenty tons of rotting monster flesh in my yard.'" Malcolm mocked Ian's voice. "You see a disaster. I see a chance to make a lot of people happy, including ourselves."

"How so?"

"Now just listen to me for a minute. Imagine a tasteful building, maybe with columns so it looks like a museum. Imagine a panoramic exhibit of the history of the loch, the monster, and the brave people who sought her. Think of the shadowy photographs, eyewitness accounts, and vague sonar readings. Then, imagine a line of velvet ropes surround Nessie, forever immortalized for us all to enjoy. Imagine children and their parents awed by nature's mysteries."

"We're not selling the monster."

"We wouldn't be. We'd be selling wonder."

"I'm not turning my home into Carcass World. If you want to make money that way, go manage a sideshow. As for us, we're going to do something about this before it scares the tourists away." Ian stood and brushed grass from the seat of his pants.

"Scares them away? You've spent too much time fishing, Ian, and you've forgotten all about people. Don't you see them lining up to see pictures of death and read stories of gore? Tourists all over the world will sell their children into slavery just to run their fingers through Nessie's entrails so they can tell the boys back at the office about it. We can give them that chance."

"What happens to everyone else on the loch if we sell the monster, Malcolm? What about them?"

"You mean the people with the tacky little souvenir stores? You mean the boat captains and their Monster Spotters? You mean Joseph McSwinney and his goddamned NessieMobile he drives all over the place? They'll work for us!"

"What about the innkeepers and restaurant owners? That creature has kept people happy and wealthy, and I'm not about to personally reap the fruits of its death at the expense of others. You may not understand that, but it's a concept we call 'honor.'"

Malcolm shook his head. "Those people sell lies and false hopes. We can sell the truth."

"You don't sell the truth. We'll give it to a museum."

"A museum?" Malcolm slapped the top of his head with his palm. "Are you kidding? Then no one makes any money. It just gets put in a drawer somewhere with a bunch of boring old bones and no one gets to enjoy it unless there's a dull tour guide along. It's not their monster, Ian. They don't know what to do with it."

Ian turned his back and walked toward the shore.

"Besides," Malcolm called after him. "Once the world finds out the monster is dead and it's in a museum somewhere, then nobody will come here anymore. Your friends will go out of business anyway. If we keep her here on the loch they still have a chance."

Ian smacked his fist against the palm of his other hand. "Goddamn it, we're not going to sell or give the creature away. And we're not going to put it in a glass case for people to gawk at."

"Then what are you going to do?"

Ian sighed. "I don't know."

Malcolm threw his hands up in the air. "You've only got a few hours until daylight, Ian. Then the whole world will see what you have in your yard. You may not know what to do, but I know someone who does. Joseph McSwinney is a man with a good eye for business. He'll make the right choice."

Ian rushed for him and grabbed him by the collar. "You do and there'll be two carcasses in my lawn."

Malcolm shoved him away. "You think about it then while I go see old McSwinney."

"But it's miles down the road. How are you going to get there without a car?"

"I'll walk. That means you've got just a few hours, Ian, to make up your mind. Are you going to seize an opportunity, or are you going to let another chance at success pass you by? The choice is yours." Malcolm strode away into the darkness.

Ian started after him, but then calmed himself and turned back where Marian had been seated before. She was gone. He looked toward the water where she stood with her arms wrapped around herself gazing across the loch.

He walked up behind her and wrapped his arms around her. "Your brother's a fool."

She nodded. "Mum always said so."

"What have you been thinking about?"

She shrugged. "I was just thinking about all those years ago when we'd sit by the water on nights like these and how you'd tell me between kisses you'd show me Nessie someday."

"I'm sorry it had to be like this."

She shrugged again. "Couldn't be helped, I suppose. I'm sorry I saw Nessie at all, to be honest with you."

"Well, not like this."

"Not at all, actually. It was always more fun to think and talk about her, to imagine she was out there watching out for us. I always dreaded the day I'd see her and she'd turn out to be a giant seal or crocodile or something."

Ian looked back over his shoulder toward Nessie. "I guess the dinosaur people were right. At least it wasn't just a log."

"It might as well be, when they're all done with her. All those instruments and measurements will make her just another dead animal specimen, won't they? She'll be like any other creature washed up on the shore. She'll answer a few questions, and then everybody'll forget about her again. She'll be in biology textbooks as a curiosity."

"It was fun to talk about her, wasn't it?"

Marian nodded. "I liked her better when she was just a possibility instead of a big, wet, clammy reality. Whenever things got too ordinary and boring, I could always think of her and the strange world she came from that I could barely feel just out in the loch."

"Maybe the tourists don't really want to see her after all. They just come for a little mystery in their lives." Ian held her closer. "We can't let them see her, can we?"

Marian shook her head, and her hair brushed against his beard.

"And we can't just roll her back in the water, either."

She continued to shake her head. "She might just float into someone else's yard, someone else who might take her and sell her themselves. I think she came here for a reason."

"Here? Why?"

"Because Malcolm was partly right about you. You are a person who faces a problem and just quietly does what it takes to get through it, no matter how difficult it is. I think she was lucky to come here to someone like you."

"How so?"

"You're the perfect person for this. You know the right thing to do and you have the strength to do it. Maybe there are whole generations of Nessie's ancestors out there in the loch, and every now and then when one dies on a night like this, they're fortunate enough to find someone like you, someone with enough spirit to understand her and enough practicality to do what has to be done. It's a special night when one of Nessie's kin comes ashore and entrusts one human to help them all live in peace and wonder."

"How do you know so much about all of this?"

"I know about Nessie because I've lived on this loch all my life and felt her every day. I know you because I love you."

"Ah. Of course." Ian held her closer for a moment.

"You know what we have to do, don't you?"

Ian nodded. "I think so."

"I'm glad she found us." Marian turned to face him and looked into his eyes.

"Me, too."

They held each other for a time before they reluctantly pulled away. Then, clasping hands, they walked toward the house. Marian smiled at her husband and he smiled back.

"Let's go get the axes."

Speaking Mouth Dog

"Moose. Indian."
— Henry David Thoreau's last words

Broman Sumner—poet, critic, raconteur—may be our nation's most precious intellectual treasure. That he started his life abandoned in a dumpster outside an Aerosmith concert makes his life even more astounding and inspirational.

Of Broman's biological parents, little is known. Boston police believe his mother, likely a crack-addicted prostitute, lurched drunkenly from her seat to sing along with "Dude Looks Like a Lady" when her infant son slapped against the concrete in a gush of placenta. According to witnesses, she nudged him beneath the bleachers until after the second encore and then left him writhing among beer cans and marijuana roaches.

Sanitation workers found the preternaturally serene trashcan Moses the following morning and discovered he was deaf, blind, mute, and addicted to crack cocaine. An outpouring of sympathy from the community ensued, and several large donors (including his namesakes at the firm of Sumner and Broman Accident Attorneys) bankrolled the trust fund that sustains him to this day.

Doomed to spend his life in a communicative void, Broman's early years were tragic ones. Because no single family could care for his physical needs, he slept in makeshift cribs at several state hospitals as a ward of the nursing staff. Elderly volunteers sang to him—futilely—

and fed him candy. Doctors offered their services for free, weaning him from cocaine and helping develop what little motor function he has today.

Not until he was sixteen years old did anyone discover the genius struggling to see through dead eyes and listen through dead ears. That person—the Columbus of Broman's continent of artistic vision—was Massachusetts Institute of Technology graduate student Gerhard Mouly, a specialist in robotics. By a miraculous coincidence, his girlfriend Julia was working on her residency at the hospital and mentioned Broman's case during their first date. Mouly, interested as he later admitted in "getting me some," recruited a team of talented friends to build the device that offers Broman his one-way conduit to the world.

No discussion of Broman would be complete without describing the device that brokers his genius to us.

Years of testing neurologically-controlled artificial limbs taught Mouly and his colleagues the intricacies of mind-motor function, technology that finds its apotheosis in the machine dubbed the SMD (Speaking Mouth Dog) by its inventors. Related only by function to the seeing eye dog, it is in essence an artificial mouth designed only for communication.

It is simplest to say that the SMD is a kaleidoscope of meaning. Electrodes attached to Broman's brain and visual cortex flash ten thousand images per second in his mind's eye, and his endorphin reaction to each is measured. Using a complex algorithm, these reactions are translated into words that are then either uttered by an electronic voice box or shown on the left or right shoulder screens on his wheelchair.

Through this interface, Broman transmits the contents of his heart. And what contents he transmits!

Lab assistants recorded his first novel, *Oatmeal! Oatmeal!* by hand during early experiments with the SMD device. This book met with considerable acclaim from graduate students for its surprising visuals, piquant social analysis, and complex linguistic structures.

Largely autobiographical, *Oatmeal! Oatmeal!* appears to be about Broman's increasing frustration with his diet of Quaker instant oatmeal.

It then soars into a metaphoric and euphoric joyride into the nature of our own daily oatmeal.

When introducing the work to her book club, Oprah Winfrey called it, "A moving tribute to the human spirit—a tour de force of unique vision and drive." The *New York Times* referred to the book as "an exciting foray into a world beyond—and perhaps behind or beneath—our own, where perception doesn't always involve the mind."

Broman dabbles in other literary forms as well, and his cycle of 4,417 haiku poems is probably the most enigmatic cycle of verse since the work of Emily Dickinson or that weird guy all dressed in black you remember from freshman Composition class. These haiku, containing two to eight line verses with up to thirty-four syllables per line, pose many interpretive challenges, not the least of which being their incomprehensibility.

Poem 161 offers a good example.

Tooth kite
Blue finger swivels Nazi homunculus
Kitchen. Crying. Lawsuit.

When interviewed about this very poem, Broman's electronic voice croaked, "Kittens!" and his left shoulder screen displayed the flag of the Ukraine. The creator of a work is seldom qualified to express its meaning: any additional discussion is but another text to interpret. Broman's work is challenge enough without his meta-textual gibbering to further distract us.

In poem 161, we have biting, flying, swiveling, and suing going on—a misogynistic vision of the common romantic relationship from love nibbles to the kitchen to the inevitable post-modern divorce.

The homunculus represents the child born of this relationship, and the poem critiques the modern love story—perhaps even of the love story of his own parents, estranged from one another and from him. If Broman is the homunculus, so too are we all the twisted, bloated fetus of our malignant society.

Since the word Nazi bears no apparent connection to the poem, we'll assume this is a syllabic place-holder, a section of bad DNA in an otherwise meaningful helix.

Prose or poetry, Broman's output may indeed be the perfect test subject for semioticians fascinated by the origins of our symbolic economy. He may be the untainted control subject theorists have been searching for: there is no tabula more rasa than his.

Broman's database contains ten million nouns, verbs, prepositions, and proper names he has no hope of ever connecting to an existing referent. When, in poem 75, he refers to "yellow orb Britney needle," we're left wondering why he chose Britney instead of, say, Blondie or Madonna. His near-sexual ode to Pol Pot would be disturbing if there were any evidence Broman knew what he was talking about.

Broman has never known love. He's never ridden the rails as a 1930s hobo. He's never kicked a football or flown to outer space or pinned two Puerto Rican transvestites to the floor in a brawl. It is therefore stunning that he has written about all of these things in such detail yet never about anything he knows firsthand, such as sitting very, very still.

Perhaps Broman's most striking skill is his use of cliché. For a person unable to have read or heard the tired phrases speckling the literary stool of lesser writers, Broman's power to invent them is extraordinary. To have reinvented expressions like "bat out of hell," "dumb as a stump," and "crazy as a shithouse rat," is remarkable since Broman has never seen bats, hell, stumps, shithouses, or rats.

We can therefore forgive Broman's second novel, *Water Animal*, for its depiction of an obsessed sea captain hunting a mysterious and near-legendary creature as an example of amazing imagination, if not the percolations of Jung's collective unconscious.

This collective unconscious may be the only intelligence he knows. There is little evidence Broman is aware of the consciousness of his audience. He may well believe that he is the only intelligent creature in the universe and that the feeding tubes and wheelchair are natural phenomena.

But then, why write? To whom is he speaking? Are words just natural body effluvia like urine or feces? If so, how does he know when he is full? Does his mouth-sphincter itch when it is time to speak?

Some claim Broman can answer questions and his responses in some way correspond to external stimuli. Journalists refuse to believe he cannot hear their questions, and his 2002 interview with local television anchor Aimee Bloom during the *Water Animal* promotional tour is a representative sample.

Instead of taking Bloom's obvious cues to plug his book, Broman chose to speak about the contents of his soul.

"Fester glass confabulation figure-skating," he cried.

"Confabulation figure skating?" Bloom glanced off stage for help. Not getting any, she recovered quickly. "What a beautiful metaphor. Such striking ones seem to—"

"Blood banjos."

"I'm sorry?"

"Rumpelstilzchen. Blue?"

The interview went on for five agonizing minutes; Bloom grinned, Broman's monitors flickered with strange insight, and the audience was left—as always—baffled. Broman again posed more questions than he answered.

For this reason, Broman may be the most popular target of critical theory alive. He is a single pulsing metaphor for Kristeva's abjection, Derrida's decentralization of textual oppositions, Freud's Oedipal issues, Marx's class conflicts, and many others. He is prime material for theses, dissertations, and articles (including this one) precisely because he embodies more questions than answers.

Most of these academic discussions of Broman require some acknowledgement of several core issues with his ambiguously performed theory of artistic creation.

What connection exists between Broman's imagined images and the words that emerge from his speakers or screens? An image of a rose, after all, can be the referent for "rose" or "flower" or "bud" or "petal" or "plant." How the SMD determines which of these words represents Broman's true intentions is a mystery even to the people who developed it, and the border between Broman's intellect and the artificial intelligence of the machine is hard to define.

Is Broman telling stories? The random structure of his narrative fiction leads several graduate students (Phillips at USC, Hulliot at the Sorbonne) to wonder if they are narratives in the strictest sense. They have no beginning, middle, or end. They are plotless, devoid of description, and indeed only have the barest caricatures of human beings as their concern.

Is Broman's work a symptom of mental illness, a plaintive wail from beneath a shell of wires and lights? Is he asking for something? And if he is, should we give it to him? What if creative genius is a function of deprivation?

Does Broman believe in God? For that matter, does Broman believe he *is* God, creating as he does meaning from darkness?

To what extent is Broman merely the servant of a patriarchal capitalist society? His machine was invented by men; it was paid for by people of wealth and privilege. Are Broman's artistic allegiances to the cultural and sexual elite?

In what genre does Broman write? *Locus* magazine calls him the "ultimate slipstream writer," referring to his use of varied genre tropes in a single work. His novella "Cowboy Rocket Murder" earned nominations for both science fiction's Nebula award and mystery's Edgar Allan Poe award.

Controversy about Broman is hardly the sole province of critics and philosophers; even software engineers explore the wild tundra of his mental landscape. There are three hundred thousand lines of C code within Broman's system: how could we detect a bug in the software? To what extent are the artificial intelligence algorithms driving the translations truly "artificial"? What quality assurance procedures did the programmers follow? Does Broman require maintenance? Rebooting? Patching? Worse, if Broman's conduit to the world malfunctioned, how would we know?

Perhaps the most significant issue surrounding Broman's life and works is whether he is alive or dead, and if that aliveness or deadness has any impact upon his art. Efforts to detect cognitive function have been inconclusive, but many critics claim the very presence of literary output indicates mental ability on some level, however debased.

Broman is cryptic when asked about these contradictions. His answers vary from "hovercraft jewelry" to "sick New Orleans," and almost every issue about him remains unsettled.

How long we'll have to harvest the fruits of his insight, no one can predict. He's already exceeded his lifespan by twenty years, and the degenerative effects of being wheelchair-bound are evident in his brittle bones. He could die at any time (if he hasn't already) and this tenuous connection to life informs his work.

In the meantime, Broman enjoys some popular celebrity. He bleated out his own national anthem at a Red Sox game recently, and his talk show appearances display skill as a pundit. Who can forget his retort to Pat Buchanan's isolationist dogma: "Jinx carrot fence spirochete"? Broman has shaken the hands of paupers and presidents, though alas, he cannot tell the difference.

Outcast from birth, a swollen battery of abuse, Broman perceives the world at a level we cannot understand. He distills meaning from chaos, and returns to us the glorious boon of wisdom—not his own, but the quiet, pulsing genius we share between us. He says what we know.

Perhaps Broman expresses it best in his most enigmatic work, poem 1281:

Hexagonal elephant lymphoma;

Pixie military

Egg.

The Trespasser

In the autumn of 1889, I had the distinct misfortune to receive a delivery of a most hideous nature, a package that would haunt my memory in retirement and stain my pride as a scientist and physician.

The horrible box was preceded by a telegram from my old school acquaintance Lord Theerian, who warned me in the wire message that I was to receive under cover of darkness an "artifact connected intimately to a very private matter" requiring my "utmost discretion and singular medical talents." Such a cryptic message served only to arouse my curiosity and it was with great anticipation that I passed the rest of the day, tending to the mundane chores of a medical professor. I sent my students home early, remaining behind ostensibly to clean and organize the instruments, and I thus engaged myself into the evening.

Late in the night, after a dramatic cloak of fog and mist had settled over the university and its environs, the large, battered crate arrived at the university medical laboratory as foretold with a fortuitous lack of public attention. The two burly, unkempt men who dragged the mammoth box into the room did so in absolute silence, and left immediately after setting it upon the nearest dissection table, without even thrusting forth a hand in expectation of a gratuity as men of their station are often wont to do. I supposed they had been paid to do this by Lord Theerian, who if nothing else had a flair for drama.

Once I heard the fading clatter of their horses' footfalls upon the cobblestones, I dimmed the gas-light so as not to draw the attention of passersby. Thus suitably shrouded in shadows, I decided to open the box, ignoring completely the letter affixed to the top. My time, after all, was strictly limited; anything described in a telegram as being "extremely unusual" should be self-explanatory and could therefore be read at a more convenient time. I cast the letter aside and advanced towards the box, hefting a prybar brought from home in my hand.

It did not escape my attention before I began my efforts to open the crate that it was five feet long and had the word "FRAGILE" emblazoned on the side in harsh, angry letters. I was chagrined to note that it had been sealed with no less than thirty nails, apparently in an attempt to discourage inspection by the railroad authorities. With a sigh and a regretful glance at my soft, uncalloused surgeon's hands, I attacked the box, wielding the prybar as I had seen others do.

After several minutes of prying, banging, chopping, and swearing, I freed the lid enough from its place to tilt it up and peer cautiously inside. I was immediately assaulted with a stench that wafted all about me as I pushed the lid back. With a titanic yawn and the snapping of nails, it fell thunderously to the floor.

By now, the smell had grown so overpowering that it took no small exercise of the will to actually look into the box. I took one last gasp of fresh laboratory air and slowly leaned over the source of the smell.

I beheld a long package carefully wrapped in canvas and glistening with some spilled fluid. My previous experience as a surgeon told me exactly what the object was, but still I was stricken with an apprehension that I could not rationally explain. After a brief struggle between my instincts and my reason, the latter proved victorious and I risked a slight tug on the canvas. It peeled away with a sticky sound to reveal a hideously distorted head of pallid, waxen flesh. The face, stretched and twisted in every conceivable direction, was frozen in an expression of supreme horror, the huge black eyes bulging wildly from the head and the lipless mouth tightened in grim resolve. A bullet hole was clearly visible above the right eye and from it oozed a milky fluid that ostensibly was the person's blood. The eyes, though, drew almost hypnotic attention from me, and I was compelled to stare into the deep wells for some time.

Despite years of autopsy experience, my lack of fortitude forced me to retreat staggering from the repulsive sight. I fortified myself with a sip from my flask and decided that a cursory glance at Theerian's letter might prove to be enlightening after all.

The letter was a long and rambling one, and I will spare the reader from its tiresome style by paraphrasing its contents here. In it, Theerian described a hunt with his friends on his country estate during which they happened to hear the high-pitched scream of some tremendous beast followed by the report of a gun. The hunters rode toward the apparent source of the sound to investigate. When they reached the barren, scorched clearing from whence the sound had come, Theerian heard something rustling in the bushes. My friend (particularly intolerant of poachers on his property) promptly fired into the foliage. Unfortunately, the person that fell lifeless from behind the brush was actually a small boy, and with much guilt Theerian dismounted his horse to investigate. The hapless victim had peculiar features and carried but one piece of luggage: an odd bag filled with rocks and leaves. It was Theerian's belief that the boy, deformed due to low breeding, was apparently turned out by his idle and loafing parents to forage for food on his own and had concluded that the large Theerian estate would be an ideal source.

A long debate with his friends and solicitor then ensued, and Theerian finally decided to send the boy to me for two reasons: first, my talents in medicine and my access to forensic facilities made me the logical choice to examine the deformed lad in the interests of scientific advancement; second, legal authorities during that time of unrest might have frowned upon the arbitrary murder of a poor vagrant boy and might have subjected Lord Theerian to troublesome and embarrassing legal proceedings.

Thus, I found myself in the possession of the corpse of a small boy and charged not only with its analysis but its disposal as well. I was unsure at that time whether I should count the delivery as a blessing or a curse. I was to find later that it was more the latter than the former, but at the time, the interests of scientific curiosity and civic duty provoked me to proceed with an autopsy. Any discovery I could make about the lad's terrible deformities might help other unfortunate souls. I immediately retrieved my notebook and instruments from their respective storage places and after washing my hands of the grit and grime that had covered the crate, I supposed myself ready to begin.

Although I was tempted to perform the operation with the subject still in the crate, I was concerned that the narrowness of the box would make precise incisions and measurements difficult. I was therefore forced to lift the body from the box and carry it to another dissection table, a task which I managed to accomplish with a great deal of difficulty. The wet canvas made the subject extremely slippery, even despite the fact that the lad was surprisingly light and frail. When I accidentally dropped the corpse to the floor, it landed with only a damp slap, instead of the dull thud of most bodies. The sagging of the sack led me to believe that rigor mortis had already set in and passed, and I was very grateful, as it meant that the organs would be well enough preserved to permit analysis of the deformed child. I retrieved my package from the floor and set it down upon the second dissection table. I then wiped some of the blood from my arms, hands, and shirt in final preparation for the actual autopsy.

I was soon ready to begin. The scant illumination forced me to draw nearer to the corpse in awful intimacy so I could see. I peeled away the successive layers of canvas, revealing as I closed in on the cadaver a slimy gray fluid mixed with his blood, which had evidently leaked during either the tumultuous transit or my own brief struggle. The blood was of an odd gelatinous nature, and it flowed slowly in little beads down the sheets of the cloth. The queer odor had dissipated in the air since I first opened the crate and it was therefore much less distracting. Although I seem to have neglected it in my notes, I recall that the smell was simultaneously sweet and bitter, reminiscent of rotting fruit.

I leaned over the top of the lad and with heavy, nervous breaths pulled the last layer away from the head. The repulsive countenance of the deformed boy appeared before me and I felt my hands slightly tremble. I regained my composure, lifted my notebook into my hand, and began to describe his head.

Three loud knocks at the door startled me from my task. They were immediately followed by a gruff shout. "Open the door! Constable!"

My heart quivered in my chest, for I knew too well the recent public outcry against grave-robbing had forced the police to redouble their efforts to thwart those repulsive yet necessary thieves. This fervor had placed more than one completely innocent anatomist at the mercy of fear and superstition, and had destroyed more than one reputation. Anxious to prevent that fate, I glanced quickly around the laboratory for a means of covering my hideous subject, and tugged a ragged blanket over his features so as to hide him from the law.

The pounding continued until I stepped up to the door. When I opened it, a portly man with a thin, spiraled mustache stood waiting. He held his lantern aloft and tried to peer over my shoulder into the laboratory.

"Good evening, constable," said I. "How can I be of service to the law?"

He glanced at me briefly and nodded a curt greeting. "I'm Constable Bidgood. May I ask your name?"

"My name is Doctor Vincent Floyd and I am a professor of anatomy at this medical school. What seems to be the difficulty?"

"We've been having some problems with body snatchers."

"Body snatchers? Surely you do not mean to intimate that I am one of their ghoulish breed?"

"Oh, of course not, sir," he said, his voice trailing off to a mumble for the final words. Then, with sudden strength, he cried, "What is that dreadful stench?"

"Stench?"

"Good God, man, surely you can smell it! It hangs in the air and seeps under the door."

"Oh," I said, pretending to suddenly understand him. "You mean the pig."

"The pig?"

I jabbed a thumb over my shoulder. "Of course. I am dissecting a pig."

"I thought this was a medical school."

"Indeed it is. We study the organs of lesser animals with similarities to our own. For instance, I've opened the stomach of the pig just now. That smell is the combined odor of stale stomach gases, rotting food, coagulating blood, and unreleased feces. I suppose the decomposing flesh of the pig isn't helping, either."

His faced turned a light shade of green. I decided to press my luck and continued. "Would you like to see it? It is a fascinating specimen, if only for its horrific deformities. The double faces are particularly fascinating, but the gnarled rear hooves have value as well."

"No, thank you, sir. Good evening."

I offered him my hand. The thick, oozing fluids that coated it shone in the flickering lantern light. "Pardon the entrails," said I.

He stared at it for a moment before turning and leaving. I nodded politely after him and securely locked the door after closing it.

With the officer dispatched, I could return to the task at hand. I began my notes with the superficial observation that he was utterly hairless and had a protruding forehead. Detailed examination of the skull showed he had an enlarged frontal lobe and slightly bulging parietal lobes which contained a brain of roughly 120 cubic inches. Exact weight and mass measurements were impossible because the tumbling bullet had rendered the brain difficult to work with as a whole. I anticipated that the anterior fontanelle would be open, which would explain the increased size of the cranium, but it was closed, and indeed showed little evidence of ever existing. Theerian's bullet had entered the left side of the frontal lobe with a hole roughly one half inch in diameter and exited through the right parietal lobe with a much bigger hole, approximately one and one half inches in diameter. The poor lad didn't even have a chance.

The hypnotic eyes that had diverted my attention before now loomed below me and I had to wrest myself away from their gaze to continue my examination. The large black orbs were so far apart they were almost on the sides of the head; I measured a three and a half inch gap between them. His nose was considerably widened compared to the normal human nose and contained a great amount of mucous, which unfortunately made quite a mess. There was a large amount of grit in it, and I hypothesized that the boy might have worked in a mine, although the dirt was of a powdery nature. The mouth was little more than a slit, and the subject's teeth were worn down to nubs, indicating that they were used more often to crush hard food than to cut soft food, and I believe the boy hardly, if ever, ate meat. Since he had no ears, I concluded that he must have been deaf to both the approach of Theerian and his companions and the scream of whatever beast had been prowling through the underbrush. For a child to be encumbered with such a grotesque face was a prospect that weighed heavily upon my mind. That he was the result of that awful inbreeding so common to the lower orders seemed certain.

Disturbed by the thought of the poor deformed lad dying a needless death, I decided to pause for a brief rest and sought refreshment from my flask. I took long, calming breaths and listened carefully to the chirping of the crickets outside. The boy remained purposefully out of sight.

Emboldened to begin again, I opted to move down and make an incision into the body cavity. I feared the boy's head might only be a grotesque prologue to the horrors contained in his fragile breast, but medical curiosity pushed me forward. My scalpel sliced through the thin gray skin easily, and the network of muscles that this incision revealed was entirely foreign to my experience. Severing the tissue from the rib cage was more difficult, and I laboriously drew the blade back and forth many times to achieve my end.

Once I had exposed the fragile, spindly frame, I exchanged instruments, choosing the smallest bone saw from my collection of equipment. It apparently was still too large, for the sternum was so brittle that it cracked almost immediately after the first stroke of the serrated blade. As I gently pulled the sides of the rib cage apart they crumbled under the force with a hollow snap. The slender ribs were now jumbled like twigs; nevertheless, I managed to count at least thirty-six of them. The need for so many became apparent as I beheld a large pair of lungs, approximately thirteen inches long and five inches wide.

Since I had never seen such deformities before, I began to suspect that this boy was not all that he seemed. I have seen in my career many clubbed feet, twisted noses, bowed legs, festering and mysterious wounds and lesions, and virtually every sort of disfiguring disease; this person, however, was of a uniform and almost purposeful peculiarity that I had never before encountered. I realized that his fragile nature made him useless for the hard labor of the working class and it was thus impossible that he was merely a vagrant. This notion came accompanied by a feeling of distinct unease.

I wiped droplets of nervous sweat off my brow and took another sip from my flask before I continued to delve further into the cavity. In order to do so, I had to pull apart the collapsing sides of the body. I managed to do this with no small amount of disgust, for the awful sound of organs slithering around in the lifeless shell as I tugged the sides disturbed my already weakened resolve. I pinned the skin to the table, folding it over twice to prevent it from ripping under the strain. With a curved clamp, I peeled one of the lungs aside and groped at what was hidden underneath. The feeble light cast little more than shadows, and it was necessary for me to position my face within a few dreadful inches of the cadaver. I leaned in, squinted, and resisted withdrawing from the fetid stench surrounding my head. My eyes widened as I fixed my stare at the hideous mockery of a heart dwelling there, wet with the remaining drops of blood, stirring gently under my shaking, prodding instrument. I looked as closely as I could, but was forced by a constitution weakened with age to look away. I dropped the scalpel and recoiled from the table with disgust.

I don't know what could have caused a heart to grow with six chambers, nor can I conjecture about the twisting purple tube that curled around the heart and wriggled reflexively when exposed to the air of the laboratory; I was certain, however, that these were not merely mutations. I had no theory as to the origin of the abomination that lay before me, but fear told me I had to get rid of it, to flee from it, to hide it away from human eyes.

Three loud raps at the door were almost enough to release me completely from the sovereignty of my senses. With a pounding heart and a quickened hand, I wrapped the thing up in the canvas again, leaving my easily replaced scalpel behind. I certainly hadn't the courage to grope for it.

"Who is it?" I demanded in a voice bereft of my usual calm delicacy.

There was no response. A glance at my pocket watch confirmed the lateness of the hour; it could not possibly have been any of the usual petty annoyances. My only guess was that the slow-witted constable had forgotten he had already spoken to me.

The duress of the situation had gotten to my nerves, I regret to confess. My usual regard for manners was swept aside as I stomped across the lab, seized the handle of the door, and yanked it open most rudely.

Between clenched teeth, I snarled, "What is it?"

There was no answer but an absolute dead stillness. No breeze stirred the bushes, no human footsteps pattered upon the streets, no insects chirped or clicked. Nothing.

From behind me in the lab, however, came a low rumbling noise like the stampede of horses. I spun to greet its cause and saw only a tightened beam of light shining through the dusty windows. It swept slowly from pane to pane and window to window until, in a realization of my deepest fear, it fixed upon the corpse of that dreadful thing.

The noise then grew louder and more highly pitched; my hands were too thin to protect my ears from the steady drone. The windows began to rattle and the floor began to shake. Shelves holding jars of carefully preserved organs collapsed, spilling their contents upon the floor.

A sudden sharp increase in the noise smashed the windows into a thousand flying diamonds. Shards spun wildly all around me, and I decided then that I was powerless to stop whatever force had invaded the lab. I ran quickly through the open door and nary glanced over my shoulder until I heard the colossal rending and splitting sound of the entire building shattering into splinters. The cracking noise echoed through the streets. I dived for cover behind a toppled apple cart. I then peered over the top to see spiraling lights soar ever heavenward, leaving behind a crumbled foundation and a pile of rubble.

The local constabulary spent several days examining the debris, even finding some of my instruments lodged in trees or thrown upon the roofs of buildings. After a protracted shrugging of shoulders and scratching of heads, local authorities finally decided that "a combination of noxious gases, animal effluvia, and a faulty gas lamp ignited the building." True, it is a decidedly implausible explanation, but I suppose it is more comfortable to our sensibilities than the truth. I certainly had no evidence to refute it.

Carefully shrouded inquiries into the possible location of any organic remains obtained no information, as I assumed they would. I knew that whatever lay in that coffin had long been retrieved by its comrades.

So, with the notes once scattered across the streets safely compiled, I have penned my account. Even though I am now able to recount these events from the calm and reasoned distance of two and a half decades, my heart is still filled with regret. I should have worked with an assistant. I should have taken better notes. I should have set aside my flask. I should have hidden the body. Given the crescendo of my horrible experience, however, I doubt that anything could have made a difference.

Yet I cannot help but wonder what astounding discovery was ruined by my recklessness. I have pondered the facts for over twenty years, and I am still unsure as to the identity or origin of the mysterious creature I examined, although I strongly believe it was not human. Anyone who, like I, had the misfortune to see the gruesome secrets beneath its skin could not conclude otherwise.

Billy

The question I'm asked over and over again by children, reporters, lobbyists, politicians, college students, activists, therapists, and all too many rat-eyed cops is, "Why do you spend so much time on the road, in protests, and in jail trying to save brainless boxes of meat?"

The answer I always provide (either kindly to a child or with defiance to a cop) is that I do it for Billy. Billy was my best friend, and the only way I could save him from your carnivorous society was to do something too horrible to bear.

I do all of this for Billy.

Given my high-profile activities against the meat industry, some people find it ironic that I grew up on a ranch in Iowa and that my father alone owned close to sixteen hundred beefboxes. He was one of the most successful ranchers in the state, and his cuts of meat won the blue ribbon at the state fair more than once.

When I grew large enough to be useful for chores, my father would send me out to feed the beefboxes. Once a day, I trotted out to the barn, dragging the cart of nutrient soup behind me, letting it splash and slosh inside. I remember the sky always being gray back then over the ranch and the stainless steel walls swallowed that grayness whole.

I'd wheel the cart into the barn and down the aisle as stacks and stacks of six-foot tall beefboxes loomed above me, each steel-framed cube of pale flesh placed in its slot and aligned in long rows disappearing into the darkness.

It was always cozy in there. The tons of living beefbox flesh surged with warm life as rows of flickering lights kept time with their every rhythm. The electrodes curling around each one hummed with latent power as they passed their impulses to each waiting block of sinewy muscle.

With their food stalks wriggling in the darkness and snuffling for the nutrient soup, I'd pull my cart from beefbox to beefbox and pour 5 liters of green slurry into each waiting orifice. "It's all in the soup, Janine. That's what makes them grow so big!" my father used to say. The beefboxes sure seemed to like it; they smelled it as soon as I stepped through the door and waved their stalks at me as I made my way from one to the next.

About halfway down the aisle on the left side lived my favorite beefbox. Most people find it hard to believe a little girl would find a friend in such a hideous creature, but I did from the moment I met him. He was the runt of the shipment; my father thought of sending him back to the nursery because he was too small.

Instead, I begged my father to let us keep him and take care of him until he grew as large as the others. My father agreed, and the task of providing extra food and care for the beefbox immediately fell to me, which I didn't mind at all.

With a child's fondness for alliteration, I called him Billy the Beefbox, and I spent hours with him every day. I'd pet his smooth, beige hide (at least what I could reach between the metal supports), sing songs to him, and sew a little sweater for his food stalk to keep it warm in the winter with his initials B.T.B. on it.

During my chores, I'd hurry and feed all the other beefboxes so I could spend the most time with Billy. I'd tell him everything that happened during my day as I fed and groomed him. He would listen and snuffle supportively until my father rang the bell for me to do the rest of my chores. Then I'd come back after I finished and talk to him until dinner.

Over the course of a year, Billy and I grew together until he bulged from his metal frame and I outgrew my fourth grade clothes.

Then my father and I had a talk that changed everything.

On an overcast September afternoon after I'd finished my chores, my father and I took a walk together across our fields to the old wooden fence on the edge of the property. When we got there, he lifted me up so I could sit and then lit his pipe. He puffed on it for a minute as the clouds passed above us.

Finally, he spoke. "Janine, you're getting to be a big girl already, aren't you?"

I nodded. "I know division now, and I can go to the library by myself, too!"

He smiled. "You sure can, and I'm proud of you. I think you're big enough now to hear something important."

"What's it about?"

"It's about Billy."

"He can live inside with us now?"

My father shook his head. "I'm afraid I've got to tell you something about Billy. I'll start with a little story, okay?"

My father always told the best stories, and I nodded enthusiastically. He swallowed hard and shuffled his feet in the grass as though he were thinking of the right thing to say.

"About a hundred years ago, there weren't any beefboxes. All of these fields were dotted with dozens and dozens of moo cows."

"Like in the zoo?"

"Just like in the zoo. Except they wandered free, eating grass all day and sleeping under trees. They weren't free for long, though."

"Why not?"

"You see, sweetie, I'm sorry to say people kept the cows and grew them so they could eat them."

"Eat them?" I crinkled my nose. "Didn't the fur feel funny in their mouths?"

My father inhaled through his teeth and winced. "Well, they didn't have their fur when they got to the people. They'd end up in slaughterhouses where machines turned them into steaks and hamburger and all sorts of other things you don't need to know about."

"Didn't people feel bad about it?"

He pointed the end of his pipe at me. "They sure did. Some people tried to argue against killing them, and others just chose not to eat the meat at all. Almost everybody tried hard to forget the dinner on their plate was once a cow."

"Yuck! That's not where our steak comes from now, is it?"

My father laughed. "Of course not. The cows are all in the zoos now or on reservations out west. Besides, the meat you have for dinner is much better than in the old days. That's the tragic part. All those beautiful animals died for inferior steaks! They had fat and gristle and germs on them. The good steaks were too expensive and the affordable ones made you sick. It was horrible."

"What did they do about it?"

"Well, some smart scientists—"

"I want to be a scientist!" I cried.

"Yes, honey. Some smart scientists just like you thought about all the sad cows and all the angry people who wanted to save them and all the unhappy people who had to eat bad food or who didn't have food at all. They used their computers and their laboratories to save the cows (and to a lesser extent, the chickens)."

"How did they do it?"

"They made cows obsolete! They used something called genetic engineering to build a special animal that had no legs, no brain (to speak of), and no messy bones. They grew these animals in big, square metal frames and gave them just the parts they needed to make good meat. They built electrical devices that would evenly stimulate their muscles for smooth, melt-in-your-mouth beef. They designed feeding stalks for nutrients and output vents for waste. They invented the perfect food animal, engineered to create a maximum of good meat with a minimum of time, space, or resources."

It began to sink in. In a strained voice I asked, "We eat beefboxes?"

My father placed a callused hand on my shoulder. "Yes we do, sweetheart. Those smart scientists fed the world with those beefboxes. They can be grown anywhere there's electricity. They make great beef, and best of all, they aren't animals. They don't feel anything at all!"

"Our beefboxes are animals! Billy is an animal!"

"No, Janine, none of them are. Remember when you were real little and you used to sleep with that old sock? You called him Teddy and went to bed with him every night. But then one day you realized he wasn't an animal but just an old sock. I'm sorry to say, love, the beefboxes are the same way."

"Then why don't any of them ever go away to be steak?"

"They do all the time. We use the forklift to load the boxes onto trucks while you're at school. You never knew because they all look the same."

I jumped off the fence and clenched my hands into tiny fists. "They do not! Billy is different!"

He sighed. "We haven't taken that one away yet because you like it so much. Now, you've fed it for so long now that it's getting too big. I guess what I wanted to tell you, Janine, is that it's going away tomorrow, and I'm more sorry about it than you'll ever know."

I started to cry. "No! No! No! He can't go away! He loves me!"

"It can't, baby. It doesn't have a brain. It just has a tiny nub that regulates the heartbeat and other body functions, but it can't think or feel anything. When it goes away tomorrow, it won't even know."

"You're a liar!" I screamed. "He's alive! He can hear me! He knows I'm coming in the mornings! Why can't we just keep him? I'll show you how smart he is."

"Because soon it's going to get too big for the box."

"Then build him a bigger box!"

"I can't."

"Why not?"

"Federal regulations provide standards for the size and we can't change them. Besides, how long can we keep it like that, honey?"

"Forever!" I threw myself to the ground, pressed my face into the soil, and howled my rage and pain into the earth. My father let me cry for a long time.

Finally, when my voice grew hoarse, he gently pulled me up and held me close against him. I heard his muffled voice through his flannel shirt.

"You can say goodbye to him tonight and tomorrow you'll have another friend. Billy has to go away now. Don't forget he and the other beefboxes save thousands of real animals every time they go and they save millions of people who would otherwise be starving all across the world. Billy and the others are heroes."

My tears began to dry on my cheeks and I wiped snot from my nose with my sleeve. He put his arm around me and I sobbed in quiet snorts and sniffles all the way home.

It was getting dark as we got near the house and my mother was waiting on the big wooden porch for us. She ran out to me and hugged me, stroking my hair and telling me everything was going to be okay.

"I know this is tough for you, but it will pass and you'll be a big, strong girl afterwards."

I nuzzled her shoulder until I smelled something in the kitchen. Hamburgers.

I pushed away from her and ran into the house, letting the screen door slam behind me. I stomped up the stairs and jumped onto my bed. There, I buried my head in the pillows and eventually fell asleep to the sound of my parents whispering to one another downstairs.

In the middle of the night, I awoke to find my mother had left milk and cookies on my nightstand, but I didn't touch either. I was afraid they'd been made out of kittens, stuffed animals, or Grandma.

I laid in bed for awhile clutching my stuffed koala and wondering what to do about poor Billy. In the morning, I'd have to go to school again, and the truck would come while I was gone and take him away from me forever.

I squinted through the darkness at the clock. 12:15. I had about six hours to save Billy but no good ideas for how to do it.

Then I remembered how Billy always listened when I needed help. Maybe he'd have some ideas on how to save us both.

I threw back the covers, tiptoed down the stairs, and opened the front door. I closed it quietly again behind me, making a tiny click as the door latched.

Across the field I padded barefoot, staying low like I'd seen soldiers do in the movies, darting from shadow to shadow under the three-quarter moon. A breeze whispered through the trees and masked the sound of my feet crunching in the grass.

I slid the steel door of the barn all the way open and I heard the movement of Billy's stalk even through the steady hum of the electrical equipment. Straining to see in the darkness, I could see it motion to me, struggling for freedom.

I knew what I had to do.

I ran down the aisle toward the equipment garage, pausing for a moment by Billy to pat him and say, "Don't worry. We're getting out of here."

Parked at the end of the barn were two forklifts. I climbed on the one the men from OSHA had said was bad because it didn't beep when it backed up, and flipped the switch as I'd seen my father do. The electric motor whirred to life.

Grasping the wheel with both shaking hands, I stomped on the pedal. The forklift lurched forward and slammed me against my seat. I struggled to hold the wheel, but it slid from my hand and the machine smashed into a rack of tools. They crashed against the floor as I kicked at the brake.

After the forklift skidded to a stop, I paused to listen for anyone coming from the house. I didn't hear anything, so I turned the wheel and tapped the pedal to drive down the aisle. The feeding stalks retreated into the boxes as I passed, the low rumble of the forklift frightening them.

I stopped beside Billy's box and used the lever to raise the forklift prongs to his level. I nudged the pedal and one prong clanged against the metal frame.

"Sorry, Billy!" I whispered, trying to be quiet.

Slowly, slowly, I inched the forklift forward until the prongs scraped into the metal sleeves of Billy's box. I stopped the machine, pulled a control lever, and raised the box out of the slot.

Somewhere I heard a dog barking. I froze, hoping the hum of the forklift couldn't be heard outside the barn.

I waited until the barking faded before I backed into the aisle and turned the forklift to face the door. Then, with Billy and I facing freedom, I pressed the pedal all the way down and sped out of the barn with the high-pitched whine of the motor echoing against those polished steel walls behind us.

The forklift bucked up and down in the grass after we emerged into the field. Billy's box rattled against the truck with every dip and jump.

I drove far out in the fields away from the house. When I could barely see the porch lights, I stopped and lowered Billy to the ground.

I backed the prongs out from the box and turned off the machine. It was suddenly silent out there in the middle of the field.

Billy's smooth, damp hide shone in the moonlight, and his feeding stalk sniffed at the open air. No more smell of barn for him. He was outside with the grass and the trees and the moon. His stalk swayed back and forth, taking it all in.

As I walked up to him, he sniffed at me. "Almost free, Billy." I patted him twice on the tattoo etched into his hide that read "8632-18970."

I began to pull wires and pins out of the frame, and metal pieces fell into the grass. On one upper corner was a yellow and black striped handle. When I jumped up and pulled it, the sides of the frame popped open and slammed into the ground. Billy was free.

He stood up straight for a second before lurching to one side with a low groan. I pushed hard to get him back up, but he was settling fast.

"You're free, Billy!" I shouted. "We can run away from here and live in the fields together. You can eat grass and I'll pet you and take care of you!"

Across the field two flashlight beams bobbed towards us from the direction of the house. My parents were coming.

"This is our chance, Billy. Run!" I sprinted away through the meadow, but I soon noticed Billy didn't follow. He gurgled and squished behind me as he collapsed further against the ground. In the poor light, I could still see his pink skin wobbling with grotesque blood vessels surging beneath. The number on his flesh became stretched and distorted.

"Run!" I screamed, but Billy didn't listen.

The flashlights were coming closer.

I ran to Billy and tried to drag him, but he was too heavy.

"Janine! Is that you?" My father called out to me.

"Billy! We have to go!"

By now I knew he couldn't. He settled into a roundish blob on the ground and strange milky fluids oozed from his sides.

I had to do something. I could see a mother buying steaks at the supermarket. I could see a family slicing Billy and serving him with mashed potatoes and asparagus and horseradish. I could see the father dabbing the corners of his mouth with a napkin and complimenting Billy on how juicy and tender he was.

I couldn't let that happen to my friend.

I jumped on the forklift and turned it on. There, quivering before me in a hunk of gelatinous flesh, was the best friend I'd ever know. In that one second, I loved more than I would ever again.

Crying and screaming at the same time, I crushed the pedal down and stabbed my friend with a forklift prong. It squished inside him, spraying blood on the forklift and splattering drops of him on my face.

With the wobbling block of flesh impaled on the prong, I gritted my teeth, closed my eyes, and yanked the wheel. The forklift spun around and tore him apart. A strange, scary popping sound cracked the air as he split into two chunks.

I was shaking so badly I almost couldn't stop the machine, but somehow I managed. My parents shouted at me from across the field, but I ignored them and ran to the remains of my friend.

I slid against the blood-slathered grass next to his feeding stalk and clasped it in my hand. He curled it around me, and I said, "I love you Billy. I'm so sorry."

Then he let go.

My father gathered me in his arms and held me close. I pounded my fists against his chest and cried, "We're not going to eat you, Billy! We're not going to eat you!"

So I wasn't born an activist, you see. I wasn't destined to travel the country, to organize protests, to write articles and broadsides, to chain myself to slaughterhouse doors, to sit in the same cold jail in a thousand little towns. I chose to do those things. I chose to do them because of Billy, because somewhere beneath those blinking lights, gnarled wires, and cold steel frame was a brain and a soul.

That's the long answer to the question of why I do all of this. The short one is that my conscience won't let me watch an ugly animal die just to save a cute one. I have to save them all. Anything else is hypocrisy.

See you on the picket line. Billy and I will be waiting.

Cthulhu Fhtagn, Baby!

Your gentle critic will grudgingly concede that he has sometimes been prone to hyperbole in his fight to protect his readers from mediocrity. True, calling *Cats* a "festering sore on the New York art scene" might have been a trifle harsh. Yes, my observation that *City of Angels* was "ersatz Hollywood trash" incited more than a few angry letters. But when I say that the new Broadway sensation *Cthulhu Fhtagn, Baby!* is the hideous spawn of dark, evil forces, rest assured I mean that literally.

You have, of course, heard of *Cthulhu Fhtagn, Baby!* The shameless marketing campaign that pumps its propaganda into the American cultural bloodstream with all the subtlety of an oil well has insinuated this Broadway show onto every newspaper page, magazine review, and television show in the country. One cannot escape its growing influence in any hair salon, book club, college class, or office break room. A person in every elevator is humming one of its memorable tunes. Normally, I shun the popular, the bourgeois, the trendy. Yet something this pervasive compels me to study it as an observer of our culture.

There is little to say about the origin or backstage politics of the play. The usual gossip that surrounds every Broadway production is oddly missing from this one. The Innsmouth Players came to town under cover of darkness in a dented rusty bus and have shrouded themselves in mystery since their arrival. The playwright listed in the playbill, Abdul Abhazred, has studiously avoided the obligatory promotional appearances. The cast has holed themselves up in the theater away from prying journalists. Even the posters are cryptic, displaying only the title and that hideous leering face.

I knew *Cthulhu Fhtagn, Baby!* was going to be a peculiar night on the town from the moment I entered the theater. A hunchbacked usher with bulging eyes escorted me (none too politely, I might add) to my seat. The crowds around me were a bizarre cross-section uncommon to the city's arts scene. Of course, the usual fashionable elite was there in full regalia; Dame Hillary von Mehren wore a stunning black dress, and her escort wore impeccable tails. Yet most of the audience were average citizens from quaint suburban neighborhoods out for a night on the town. Also in attendance but from further down the economic food chain were the blue-collar rabble from across the river. Apparently there for the sheer spectacle of the show, they tittered and whispered nervously in the unfamiliar surroundings and were most rude. Eventually, however, the diverse crowd settled into their seats and the show began.

I must admit that the plot was certainly a clever twist on the traditional boy-meets-girl story. The male lead character is Franklin Whipple, a dashing young professor of antiquities at Miskatonic University. He is drawn from his solitary, academic life of personal genealogical researches and occult dabbling by the charms of a deceptively beautiful woman. During a bicycle tour of the smaller Massachusetts hamlets he discovers the seductive Gretchen, who to his idealistic eyes looks like the very figure of purity and goodness. His heart deceives him, however, as we in the audience soon discover that she happens to be the illegitimate demi-human spawn of the great evil Cthulhu. Her sole purpose on the Earth is to complete the foul marriage of the human race with the shambling, pestulent alien overlords from the dark corners of the galaxy.

A tragic series of events ensues. I wouldn't normally spoil the end of the show for my readers, but since it is my sincere hope that you avoid this one at all costs, I will do so. After a few fitful starts and stops, the petty arguments and jealousies of young lovers give way to a passionate romance between the two. Whipple refuses to believe the gathering series of signs that he is in trouble: his lover's predilection for raw fish, her bulging eyes, the passages of the Necronomicon she quotes tenderly in love letters. With the inevitability of destiny, the play concludes with the terrible wedding of Franklin and Gretchen (the father, incidentally, does not give her away) and the subsequent grisly murder of Franklin upon a stone altar of blasphemy. With a spray of blood into the first three rows of the audience and a howling scream that echoes through the theater, she then clinches the destruction of the human race, devouring his flesh during a crescendo of song and dance.

The music that warbled from the Erich Zann Orchestra during this spectacle was as horrible as the events on the stage; its melodic structure and tonal quality had all the musical majesty of a toppled china cabinet. The songs, from the baldly derivative "Don't Cry For Me, Miskatonic," to the strangely familiar "Ode to Dagon," mercilessly abused my musical sensibilities. The pulsing rhythms of the "March of Rhan Tegoth" are not for a normal number of marching feet.

Costuming was another weak point. Oily sequined fish scales comprised most of the women's costumes, evoking images of West Virginian prom nights. The dresses stretched to coat every ill-placed lumpy curve of the slimy dancers. Gretchen's tattered rags were designed by the same person who dresses our city's homeless. Whipple's wardrobe, evidently resurrected from Grandpa's attic trunks without an intervening trip to the laundry, hung on the actor like a ragged set of curtains. Every local thrift store must be empty.

The less said about the acting, the better. The actress who played Gretchen overdid the part with an intensity apparently studied at the Charles Manson School of Wild-Eyed Staring. The actor who played Whipple, the sixth to do so in as many performances, was so obviously ill-prepared for the role that his death would have been utterly unconvincing without the gore. The supporting cast was similarly dreadful; the dancers stomped and wriggled like epileptics, the so-called monsters drooled and staggered like drunks. The cast was, to a man, incompetent and amateur. They shouldn't be doing high school Shakespeare, much less Broadway.

In every measurable, objective quality, this show was quite probably the worst to ever appear before human eyes. One need not spend eight years in Europe studying the form as I have to know that this play is dreadful. To preserve the decency and prestige of the stage, this travesty should be pulled from the theater and all involved should be publicly shamed.

Yet every show is sold out, and my night was no exception. Even more disturbing than the show itself was the reaction of the audience. From the first scintillating undulations of the Innsmouth Chorus Line, the audience sat entranced. The emotional tenor of the room slavishly rose and fell with the moods of the play, and the collective unconscious of all present swirled and frothed at the stirrings of those players. Never before have I seen spectators so involved with a show. They were transformed at the beginning of the first act from an audience to a congregation.

They were most disturbing at the end of the show. While my stomach was turning and only journalistic integrity prevented me from bolting from the theater, they stared with rapt attention at the vicious slaughter of Franklin Whipple and indeed cheered on the evil woman who did the deed. With every thrust of the knife, they leaned closer. They drooled, licking their lips and wringing their hands in starving anticipation.

The restless excitement of the crowd became a frenzy after the climax of the play. When the curtain finally and mercifully dropped, the crowd rose as a single massive creature from their seats chanting "Ia! Ia!" Gnashing their teeth with primal rage, they pushed their way through the crowd with a low growl, and emerged from the building in a great blood-thirsty horde. I could barely hear someone in the lobby screaming for salvation that would never come over the din of their march.

Only my formal training in theater allowed me to resist the hypnotic presence of the play and the mass psychosis of the audience. Using my cape to shield me, I managed to squirm through the crowd and escape into the nearest cab. As the taxi pulled out of sight, all I saw behind me were hundreds of people flooding into the streets, kicking over garbage cans, smashing store windows, and assaulting passersby. They were not a Broadway crowd any longer.

This show isn't simply bad; it is evil. It is profane even by current standards, and watching it can very literally be damaging to the health. To borrow a metaphor from two of my less sophisticated colleagues, I cannot thrust enough thumbs down far enough to convey the utter horror of *Cthulhu Fhtagn, Baby!* At the very least, the show is profoundly disturbing, and I believe the disclaimer in the playbill that children under six should be forbidden to attend is somewhat understated. This show is not meant for human eyes.

I implore my readers to avoid this show and the merchandising that surrounds it like a thundercloud at all costs. Boycott the upcoming animated film, television show, and soundtrack album. Do not purchase the Cthulhu action figure with spring-loaded facial tentacles. Shun the stuffed animals, dolls, board games, T-shirts, commemorative plates, breakfast cereals, collector's programs, and candy bars that have sprung forth from this monstrosity like spores. Every dollar spent on merchandise only encourages them. If you heed but one of my critical warnings, follow this one. Much more may be at stake than two wasted Broadway tickets.

Soured

Brandon hated milk: the texture, the taste, the soggy sludge it left in the bottom of his cereal bowl. When his mother slid a glass across the greasy Waffle House table, he crinkled his nose and repressed a gag.

"Drink it, honey," said Mom, now digging in her purse.

"I don't want to. It gives me diarrhea."

"No, it doesn't."

"I'll bring you some next time."

"Don't be gross." Mom pulled out a pill bottle and twisted off the cap. "Just drink it, Brandon. Your bones are going to be foam rubber if you don't. You'll have a Nerf skeleton." She tipped a tablet in her mouth and swallowed it dry.

The glass door of the restaurant slammed closed. A few bleary-eyed truckers glanced over as Brandon's father staggered inside blotting sweat from his forehead with a Wet-Nap.

He slid into the booth next to Brandon.

"What did you find out?" Mom sipped her iced tea.

His dad sighed. "According to the yokel at the garage, the axle is broken. I don't know how that could have happened on these medieval Florida roads."

"Can they fix it?"

"They won't be able to get an axle for a Winnebago in less than three days." Brandon's dad flipped over the plastic menu, shaking his head. "What the hell's the difference between 'smothered' and 'covered' hash browns?"

"We're not staying here for three days!"

"I told him to weld it so we can limp to an exit with technology from our century and that's what they're going to do."

Brandon tugged on Dad's sleeve. "My robots are in the camper. Should I get them now?"

"What?" Dad frowned. "You'd better hurry; it's going up on the rack shortly."

Brandon squirmed under the table and ran out into the beating sun of the desolate freeway exit. Grit-covered cars and trucks rested in rows in the gravel parking lot while gas pumps groaned.

Brandon circled behind the gas station toward the camper but froze when he saw what was parked beside it: a milk tanker truck.

His stomach turned. That truck might be filled with white goopy milk, warming in the heat. He tried not to think about it as he stepped closer to his family's camper, passing the truck without taking his eyes from it.

A splash echoed inside.

Brandon stopped. Could that have come from the truck? No. Someone spilled some gas or turned on a hose to spray insects off a windshield.

He stepped closer and pressed his hand against the tanker. A vibration wriggled through his arm to his spine.

Something bumped against his hand.

Brandon yanked it away. He stumbled backwards and then scrambled to the camper. He fumbled with the latch and dove inside.

He peered out through the Plexiglas window to see if anyone else had noticed. A trucker dropped from the cab like cookie batter and tried to pull his loose-fitting pants over his bulging gut with no effect. If he heard whatever was inside the truck, he paid no notice and waddled into the convenience store.

Brandon grabbed his transformable robots from his bunk and crouched under the folding dining table. His mind raced through all the possibilities. Did something else make the noise? Did he just imagine the splash, the quiver, the shuddery feeling?

Or was something living inside the truck?

A sharp rap startled Brandon into a scream. A man in coveralls lurched into the camper holding up his grimy hands.

"Kid! Kid! Calm down, for Christ's sake. We're taking the camper away to fix it. You have to get out now."

"There's something in the milk truck!" Brandon pointed.

The mechanic glanced over his shoulder. "Probably milk."

"No," whispered Brandon. "Something else."

The mechanic scratched his head. "Sorry, kid, but I don't have time to play. Your old man is yelling words at me I didn't even know existed. Why don't you go tell your mama about the milk truck?"

Brandon hated when adults said things like that. He gathered his robots and stalked outside with haughty dignity.

The workmen towed the camper away as Brandon stood staring at the truck. He knew what Mom would say if he told her: it was just his imagination. The gnomes? Just his imagination. The alien spaceship? Just a balloon or a kite or an airplane. The six suited men following them in the subway during their vacation in Washington? Just executives on their way to work.

He couldn't tell Mom without evidence.

Clutching his robots, Brandon stepped toward the truck and paused every few feet to listen. Every time it was silent he took a step forward, and every time he heard something shuffling inside that metal chamber he stopped.

Maybe it's just a cat, he thought. Someone left the top open and a thirsty cat fell in.

Just to be safe, he unfolded one of his toys into an attack mode and the little gun glowed. The robots would protect him.

Brandon made it to the ladder that curled from the side of the truck to a large valve on the top. He reached for it, and the steel was cold. He stowed his robots in his pockets and began to climb.

"Goddamn it!" A voice bellowed behind him. "Get off my truck!"

Brandon dropped to the ground. The trucker stood by the corner of the store, his teeth askew, his face covered with a speckled beard. He held a concrete block with the word MEN painted on it and a key chained to one end.

"What do you think you're doing? That truck isn't a jungle gym! You want to get me sued?"

Brandon shook his head and backed up.

"Yeah, I'll bet. Now you get the hell out of here before I call the cops!"

The trucker waited as Brandon backed away from the truck. Then, shaking his head, he stepped behind the building.

As soon as the trucker was out of sight, Brandon scrambled up the ladder again. He knew the man wouldn't be in there for long and he had just a few short minutes to find out what was banging around inside. He made it to the top seconds after he heard the latch close on the restroom door.

With all his strength, Brandon tugged on the valve wheel. It turned slowly, and he kept at it.

Inside the truck, something gurgled.

Brandon stopped, swallowed, and then continued turning the wheel. I'm just going to look inside, he thought. Then I'm running for it.

The valve stopped. The hatch was unsealed. Brandon tipped the cover back and then leaned forward to peer inside the milk truck.

It was dark and empty. Brandon unfolded another robot and a yellow beam shone from its head. He reached down into the tank and pointed it at the sides.

Milk residue slid down and gathered at the ends of the tube. The intense smell of warm milk nauseated Brandon like breathing from a milkshake-filled scuba tank.

The light glinted against the steel and something shuffled into the shadows.

Brandon traced the beam along a single pink tentacle and found its owner: a pale squid-like creature blinking a single glaucoma-grayed eye at him.

He stifled a scream so the trucker wouldn't hear.

The thing thrashed, milk festering in sores along its limbs, mouth suckling at the sides of the truck.

Brandon pulled away from the hatch. Mom would take care of it. He'd describe the monster and tell her it was inside the truck and she'd find it and make it go away.

Mom would take care of it.

He reached over to the hatch and started to close it but a moist tentacle snapped from inside and clasped around his wrist.

Not caring about the trucker anymore, Brandon screamed for help, his cries a torrent of nonsense words to anyone if they'd been close enough to hear them: "Help! Tentacles! In the milk! In the milk!"

The squid-thing pulled harder, strengthened by gorging on thousands of gallons of milk. Brandon slammed the hatch lid down on the limb and orange blood sprayed across his face.

The creature shuffled from its corner and entered the sunlight. Its huge marbled head glistened with moisture and its eye blinked to see.

The thing yanked Brandon inside the milk truck, clubbing his head against the rim and slamming him with a metallic throb against the steel. Milk smeared across Brandon's face and hair while his sobs echoed in the container.

The creature slurped and drew Brandon closer. A black tongue swirled around its maw as it sopped up milk with Brandon's helpless body.

Brandon blinked, dazed. He gouged his nails into the tentacle but didn't even slow it down. He wrested his right hand free, and Brandon knew he had one chance. He tore a robot from his pocket and clenched it in his fist.

Just as the creature's eye widened in anticipation, he stabbed the robot—and its sharp chrome gun—straight into the orb.

"Watch your eyes with that damned thing," Mom always said.

His hand squished into the gelatinous eye. The thing screeched and flailed inside the tank, loosening its grip. He snatched his arm away and jabbed the toy over and over and over again until the orb washed out into the puddle of milk. The creature gurgled and writhed in its own gore.

Brandon caught his breath and screamed again for help. The creature slammed against the tank until it groaned and then fell silent.

An arm reached down inside the tank and yanked him from his prison by the collar.

"Did you kill it?" The trucker lifted him in the air. "I told you not to go in there!"

Brandon tried to wriggle from his grasp but the trucker was too strong. The man carried him kicking into the Waffle House.

"Who owns this kid?"

Brandon's dad slid out of the booth and rose. "He's my son. Put him down."

The trucker dropped Brandon and he ran crying to his mother's lap.

"What the hell is going on?"

"That boy climbed into my milk truck and killed my Graeth'ka!"

"Oh, sweetie," said Mom, petting Brandon's hair.

"There was a monster in the truck," he said, gasping between sobs. "It tried to eat me. It looked like an squid."

Dad sighed and pulled out his wallet. He withdrew a card and handed it to the trucker. "I'm sorry, mister. The boy didn't know any better. Call my practice first thing Monday morning and I'll arrange to pay for it."

The trucker snatched the card from his hand. "You better watch your kid more carefully."

"And you'd better lock your tanker."

The trucker grunted and pushed his way out.

"Mommy!" Brandon cried. "It was a monster."

His parents exchanged a look.

"Oh, no, dear," Mom said. "It's not a monster. Those creatures help us to make the milk better! They drink a little milk and then good juices flow from their skin. Those juices make growing boys strong, tall, and smart!"

Brandon pulled away. "They're in every milk truck?"

Mom held him close. "Honey, there's a little one in every jug."

He fell back from the table.

"They make the milk better, Brandon," said Dad after sipping his coffee. "We give them a little milk and they give us better health. They're good to have around, like spiders."

Brandon knocked over his glass and it shattered against the floor. Something white skittered under the booth.

Brandon ran outside. Before the door closed behind him, Dad's voice followed him into the sunshine.

"Wait until he finds out what's in hot dogs."

Portrait of the Horror Artist as a Young Man

Dad, phone wedged against his shoulder, took a drag from his cigarette. "Principal Hoskins there?"

Todd slid against his doorframe. Please let him be gone for the day already. Please.

"I'll hold." Dad set the orange juice on the counter and took down a glass.

"Hoskins?" He stooped for the vodka beneath the sink. "Tom Albritton, Todd's father. We just got his report card."

Todd winced.

Dad poured a generous portion. "Here's my question." He splashed in some orange juice and took a sip. "How does anybody get an N in fucking Art?"

Dad held the phone away.

"Whoa! Nothing wrong with the word 'fuck.' Your parents even did it once."

An angry buzz crackled from the phone.

"Okay, lighten up." Dad puffed his Marlboro. "Give me a fucking N in poise," he growled beneath his breath.

"Art's subjective, right? Guys painting toilets make a killing. How is anything above feces on a tile worth less than an A?"

Principal Hoskins explained. Todd's shoulders tensed. Once his father knew what'd he'd done—

Dad removed Beefaroni bowls from the sink. "Uh, huh," he said, unzipping his pants. "Right." Urine splashed against the rubber garbage disposal flaps.

"He drew what?"

Todd covered his face. Here it came: the Turning. Screaming and hitting, a class ring scratching his face. Then sobbing in the dark.

Dad shook himself.

"That's it?"

Todd peered between his fingers.

"He drew a werewolf devouring his teacher?" He stroked his beard. "It was good, right? What's the problem?"

Dad snorted. "Horrific? Here's horrific." He zipped. "My twisted kid's got more imagination than you'll ever have. He'll make more money and get more ass. Better ass. Symmetrical ass.

"Let me guess: you're forty-five with permed hair and big brown glasses, right? No woman has ever squealed, 'Plow me deeper, Principal Hoskins.' You've never smoked a joint or climbed into the girls' dorms. You've never felt a surge within your veins: your blood is cold and now you're trying to chill my son's. Fuck that."

He ducked under the cord.

"If he ever comes home with clean fingernails, combed hair, and wholesome can-do attitude, I'll brain him with a bottle of Sutter Home and dump his carcass in the woods." His cigarette flared an exclamation point. "And he'd damned well better do the same for me."

Dad slammed down the receiver and gulped his screwdriver. He flipped his ice into the sink and started down the hall. Todd scrambled, pretending to pick up his clothes.

Dad's hairy hand rattled the doorknob and the door swung open.

"I'm only going to say this once."

Todd closed his eyes.

"Next time you draw a werewolf tearing someone apart, make that jackass clear as a photograph. Got it?"

Todd nodded.

Dad looked down at his watch. "It's goddamned four o'clock. Go out and play, already." Grinning with yellowed teeth, he mussed Todd's hair. "Knock over Mrs. Olney's gnome statues again and be back by seven, okay?"

Todd wriggled from his grasp and ran.

Raw Recruits

March 9, 1863

Dear General Asquith,

I have been pleased to serve my country and its noble cause against the Southern agitators, and (like any gentleman officer) I am accustomed to using the advanced skills of my education and breeding to further our struggle. Most of my contributions, therefore, have not in fact been on the field of battle in desperate combat with the enemy but instead have been in the ancient field of intelligence.

Wars are won and lost with information, sir; you may rest assured of that. Whispered rumors of troop movement, higher battlefield perspectives, and broken codes are all tools with which enemies are defeated. Whatever moral differences exist between combatants in a conflict, the success or failure of either side relies heavily upon the advancement of brilliance of one over the other.

In the past, I have suggested many successful schemes to gather information about our enemy. As you may recall, I proposed the use of aerial balloons to provide advanced battlefield perspectives. I encouraged the questioning of escaped Negroes for their knowledge of Rebel movements and conditions. I developed a network of spies in several port cities to locate British ships evading our blockade. My newest plan is sure to bring swift success and great benefit to our forces, if you are willing to excuse its eccentricities.

Perhaps I should explain the sequence of events that led me to my plan before I detail it for you. An understanding of the background might lend greater context to my scheme.

Several days ago on a mild spring afternoon, my adjunct Lieutenant Lewis and I happened to be inspecting the recently occupied Sharpsburg when we chanced upon a curious shop in the neglected section of town.

"Look, General," said Lewis, pointing at its filthy facade. "A fortune teller."

Emblazoned on the glass in wavering chalk letters were the words, "Madame Darque, prognosticator, fortune teller, love advisor."

"Indeed, Lewis. What of it?"

"I was wondering, sir, if it might be a pleasant afternoon's amusement to engage Madame Darque's services. I would like very much to see such a person perform her charlantry."

I checked my watch. Our rendezvous with the 23rd Company wasn't for another two hours, so we had plenty of time for such an excursion. We entered the shop forthwith.

Hanging from every conceivable surface in the tiny shop were the assorted accoutrements of the occult: jars, vials, dusty books written in long forgotten languages. In the center of the room was a small table surrounded by three chairs, and the withered hag that hunched behind the table was a frightening sight. Her face, creased and leathery, contorted into a perpetual sneer, and her eyes were dull and cloudy. She reeked of rotting food, cheap whiskey, and a profound stench of desiccation.

"Good afternoon, gentlemen," she rasped as we gazed at the shop in stunned silence. "Looking for something?"

"Not particularly, madam," I replied, hefting a shrunken head in my hand. "We weremerely interested in some of your curiosities."

"Ah," she said, leaning over her table. "Higher spirits led you here."

I smiled. "Of course they did. Rum and scotch, mostly."

She didn't seem to be listening to me but gazed instead at Lewis as he rummaged through a box of tiny animal bones. "I see your pain from here, gentle sir. Someone close to you has died, yes?"

Lewis stopped. Slowly turning to face her, he said, "What makes you say that, madam?"

The woman stared him intently in the eye. "I can see things beneath the skin, things you do not know yourself. My senses are tuned to the subtle vibrations of the universe, and I feel emanations from you of great anguish."

Lewis stepped closer to her. I chuckled at his naiveté.

"What do you know of it?"

She rubbed her knobby fingers across a dusty glass sphere. "I see a lost one. A father, a brother..."

"Father? Brother? Wait! My father's brother! My uncle!" cried Lewis, surging toward her. "Can you hear him?"

She nodded slowly. "He's calling to you from beyond. He wants desperately to talk to you."

Still smiling, I reached for Lewis's elbow, "Come on, lieutenant. Don't let the woman agitate you. She is clearly a talented actress."

Lewis pulled away from me and sat down in the chair in front of Madame Darque. "What does he have to say?"

"Lewis, it is time to go," I said walking toward the doorway, but he didn't seem to be listening to me.

The woman took both of Lewis's hands in her own and gazed into his eyes. Then, in a voice quite unlike her own, she said, "Eddie, boy, be a good lad and check the planks in the northeast corner of the barn. I've hidden some money there to take care of your aunt and mother if anything ever happens to me."

Lewis quivered in his chair. "I'll send word at once to Mother and instruct her as you say. Tell me, uncle: what awaits us beyond the veil?"

The woman's voice suddenly became soft and flowing in a fashion entirely opposed to her grizzled physique. "Glory, my boy. Glory." Her voice faded into silence. I became aware that moment that every sound and sight in the room had been obscured as though frozen in time. I could scarcely breathe.

All three of us sat quietly for almost a full minute before I felt compelled to break the stalemate. "Lieutenant, we have duties."

"Yes, sir," said Lewis dazedly as he rose from the chair. He pulled a wad of uncounted bills from his pocket and set them before the supposed sorceress.

"Thank you." His manner seemed too earnest for my taste.

The woman bared her gnarled teeth in an approximation of a smile. "You're quite welcome, young man."

With great relief, Lewis and I emerged from the shop a few seconds later safely among the company of the living. I couldn't decide if I should comfort the clearly shaken lad with the sharp reason of skepticism, so I opted to remain silent for the rest of our walk to camp.

Several days later after I had convinced Lewis that the entire affair was nothing more than an elaborate hoax, he came to my room with news from his family. With the instructions provided by Madame Darque, Lewis's mother did indeed uncover a considerable treasure beneath the barn and remitted a good portion of the cash to him. It was then that I began to believe that Madame Darque might actually be a talented seer and communicator with the beyond.

The full implications of this communication with the dead did not impress themselves upon me until last night. You see, General, the deciding factor in war is the advent of new weaponry and battle techniques. The clumsy weapons of yesterday's wars are not suited for the pursuit of victory in our modern conflict, and it is therefore necessary that we employ new and unusual techniques to defeat the enemy. Hence, I believe that the weapon that will bring us certain victory is a legion of ghostly spirits recruited from heaven to use their skills on the behalf of our just cause.

The advantages of employing the dead are manifold. Among the ignorant and superstitious Southerners, a ghostly apparition on the battlefield could be a powerful tool in breaking their will. The morale of our own men will be vastly improved by the knowledge that even death itself cannot stop the Union army. Having already lost their lives in battle, these ephemeral forms are invulnerable to any worldly weapon. They are capable of traveling at great speeds and through solid matter, and their general ability to hide themselves from living eyes makes them the perfect spies. In short, these soldiers can be invaluable to our army by returning to its service from beyond the grave.

I propose to use the formidable skills of Madame Darque to contact these soldiers and recruit them to again raise arms against the enemy. They will gladly fight again for that which they spent their lives so willingly. The coddling comforts of distant Aidenn are of no importance to a soldier with a thirst for glory in his veins, and I daresay that any man truly in the service of his nation never considers his duty entirely completed.

More specifically, Lieutenant Lewis and I intend to approach Madame Darque on Thursday of next week to begin our first attempt to contact our men. I intend to take command of as many spirit volunteers as possible and test their abilities in a simple intelligence gathering operation. Once we have determined their willingness and suitability for our tasks, a coordinated effort with their help can be carefully orchestrated by our superiors.

Of all of our commanders, I know that you possess the singular foresight and courage to take full advantage of this opportunity, and I am honored to bring it to your worthy attention. Please inform me when you would like to proceed.

Sincerely,
General Peppenhorst

April 18, 1863

Dear General Asquith,

Thank you, sir, for the prompt remittance of both your permission and your financial backing to my intelligence enterprise. I am attaching to this epistle a fully detailed report of my expenses with a slight deficit for which I compensated from my own savings. No price is too great to win this war, and my life and wealth are at the disposal of our Union.

In your letter, you requested a full report of my activities along those lines, and I provide here an account of our initial explorations into the realm of the dead.

Lewis and I visited Madame Darque in the early morning a week ago. The shop was as we left it: old, filthy, and on the verge of collapse. With Union money tucked safely into the pocket of my coat, we entered the shop.

Madame Darque was finishing with one of her customers. The lanky gentleman stood from the table as we entered, tossed her a few coins, and said, "Contact me if you hear anything from them."

"I certainly will, sir," said she, as her gnarled claw-like hand scraped the coins from the table into a waiting box.

Rudely, he strode past Lewis and I without even a greeting and allowed the door of the shop to slam behind him.

Madame Darque shook her head. "You must pardon him, gentlemen; he's about to receive grave news."

"Indeed," I said, straightening my coat. "I daresay we all have heard grave news in these times."

She nodded. "Have you returned for a reading?"

I glanced at Lewis. "After a manner of speaking, ma'am, yes. As you can probably tell without the benefit of arcane powers, we are representatives of the Union army."

"I had gathered that."

"We are charged here with a mission of great importance involving your singular skills and abilities."

"Really? And what would that mission be?"

I cleared my throat. "We intend to contact our fallen comrades with your assistance and enlist their aid as spies for our cause."

She looked down at her table for a moment of introspection. "What you ask of me may be considered by some of my colleagues as unethical. We who study the arts of the world beyond are not interested in the fleeting squabbles of the Earth. I am not certain that I can help you."

"Unethical?" I was stricken by the irony of those words escaping from her mouth. "How long, madam, have you told the gentleman who just left that more information is coming tomorrow, if only he'll pay a little more? It seems to me that the borders of ethics are somewhat less than well-defined in your profession."

"Isn't that the way it always is, General?"

"Not always. Our present conflict is one of clear sides of dark and light. We offer you the chance to choose something other than moral ambiguity and personal gain."

"Dark and light, you say?" she asked with a strange grin.

"Yes."

"With no personal gain?"

"Well, actually, we are prepared to pay you for your services."

"I double my normal rate."

"Double it? Whatever for?" Lewis demanded.

She turned to him. "I've never contacted so many spirits before. I cannot say what the effect will be upon me."

Lewis and I looked at each other. "Oh, very well," I said, tossing the cash on her table. "You may retain any surplus as a gratuity. Consider it a payment for your discretion, if you follow my meaning."

"I always do, General." She scooped the money off the table and tucked it in her pocket. "Are you ready to begin?"

"I am indeed." Lewis and I sat down in the two battered chairs across from her, and she began her work. She crushed some herbs, shook some sort of rattle, and swayed her head from side to side as Lewis and I looked on.

For several minutes, she muttered vague, slurred words to the collection of trinkets. She stroked the crystal ball with great care and fondness. Although I saw nothing at first, she apparently received some indication from the netherworld, for she looked up after a short while and said, "They're ready to hear you now, General."

I cleared my throat. "Gentlemen? Is anyone there? Fall in!"

Nothing seemed to happen.

"They seem reluctant to come forth, General. Perhaps you might say some words to inspire them."

I expected as much. I nodded, rose from my seat at the table, and lifted my hands to the heavens. "Men, I'm sorry to disturb your peaceful repose in the fields of the Lord, but we poor wretches upon the Earth require one last service from you all. As you well know, our fragile human bodies aren't always up to the tasks required of us in battle, and sometimes we are required to call upon higher forces. We've prayed consistently to our Lord in heaven for decisive victory as quickly as possible, and our answer has yet to arrive. We therefore call on you, our emissaries in the domain of God, to help us in this time."

The old woman nodded and grinned.

I continued. "We need you now to be our ears and our eyes, to listen to the stirrings of the human mind and help us predict the motions of the enemy. Stalk their camps, listen to their whispers, and peer at their maps. Tell us all that you see and hear. Any intelligence you can provide may be what makes the difference between victory and defeat.

"Those are your orders. You are dismissed."

I settled in my chair heavily, exhausted by my speech. The swirling colors of the crystal ball seemed to darken, and Madame Darque laughed aloud. "You've stirred them, General. They are donning their uniforms for their final battle. They march! They march!"

Lewis started backing toward the door, and I soon decided to join him. The woman seemed to be veritably writhing with strange enthusiasm, shaking and shrieking and swinging her arms in the air. The table tottered violently and a smell of sickly rot filled the air.

"They are on the march for you, General. I will give you their word when they send it."

"We'll be waiting for it. Remember that you have been well paid for your services."

"And you will get every penny's worth, I assure you, sir."

Being perhaps a bit abrupt, I nodded curtly and Lewis and I departed the shop. We all but dove into the warm and welcome street. Never before has sunshine been such a soothing sight. We both felt the oppressive aura of our experience slowly dissipate in the presence of crowds and busy streets, and we walked solemnly back to our quarters.

It didn't take long for our response. Six days later, Lewis received a note from Madame Darque with our first message. To continue the experiment, I propose that we act upon it this information during our current campaign for Chancellorsville. Given the sensitive nature of the information, I have chosen to remit it under separate cover.

I await further orders, General.

Your obedient servant,
General Peppenhorst

April 18, 1863

General Asquith:

Our message from Madame Darque reads: "Weak and tired men wait for Union death on the ridges of Salem Church. They intend to rest for another fortnight, but will then be reinforced and prepared for battle."

The message seems entirely clear. I suggest to the general that we should attack these forces immediately, preventing them from restrengthening. Please send complete orders as soon as you decide how to proceed. I look forward to another victory for our cause.

Sincerely,
General Peppenhorst

May 1, 1863

Dear General Asquith,

You message has been received. I am forwarding your orders to Sedgewick and the VI Corps. May the glory of our forces be the glory of the Lord. I will inform you of further developments when our task is complete.

Sincerely,
General Peppenhorst

May 10, 1863

Dear General Asquith,

Permit me to extend my sincerest apologies and sorrow for the loss of your sons in the disastrous battle of May 4. You will be proud to know how valiantly they fought against incredible odds. It is said among the men that Edward continued to fight despite his many wounds and was only finally felled by a cowardly cannon shot. They were the only hope we had in a hopeless battle.

As for the gross miscalculation of forces and odds by our intelligence network, I have no rational explanation. I reread the message for any misunderstanding and found none. I have investigated the possibility that rebel spies exchanged one message for another, but I have found no evidence of this.

The only answer I could find for this horrific incident comes from the hag herself, and it is an answer that is insufficient for my tastes. I offer it here only to complete my report and dissuade you from future research in the area of spiritual espionage.

Soon after exhausting every other venue of research, I chose to confront the woman herself and demand an explanation. Lewis and I stormed into her shop yesterday morning and caught her by surprise. Her crystal ball was covered on a shelf and her table was clear of the tools of her trade. She was clinging to a ladder and reaching for something upon a high shelf.

"You!" I cried, slamming the door behind me. "We demand satisfaction for your miserable failure."

"Failure?" said she, climbing down from the ladder with a book in her hand. "Failure? I'm sorry, General, but I was entirely successful."

The volume of my voice grew with my anger. "How can that be? Your information was wrong. That army wasn't tired or weak. It had already been reinforced, and we merely marched to our destruction! The VI Corps was lured by your words into a trap. Thousands of men died! Thousands were slaughtered on your lies and evil! Thousands of fathers, brothers, and sons are now lost forever to the world!"

The crone tilted her head toward me. "Lost forever to this world, perhaps, General. But not to the others. The North and South aren't the only forces gathering for battle and recruiting armies."

Lewis and I were struck speechless. After a brief silence, the woman continued. "The insignificant battles with which you concern yourself are nothing compared to the vast struggles of a universe that you cannot understand. The petty skirmishes of the material world are only training grounds for the true war in which your men will make excellent servants."

I shivered involuntarily with sudden understanding. "You deliberately marched our men into certain death to serve you?"

She shook her head. "Death is not quite what you think it is. Your men merely marched onto another battlefield under the command of more powerful officers. Smarter ones, too."

There was nothing left to say. I had my answers, and my anguished soul enabled me to see only a single recourse. I raised my cavalry pistol and aimed it squarely at her head. With every intention of relieving that vile hag of whatever she deigned to call brains, I cocked the hammer and curled my finger around the trigger.

"Sir," said Lewis. "You might be ill-advised to do that."

I paused for a moment.

Lewis continued. "What happens when she dies? Are we truly destroying her, or are we merely promoting her to the command of a great army?"

My gun wavered. "Damn," I said under my breath. I lowered the weapon to my side.

"Your lieutenant is wise indeed, general."

I pondered what to do for a few moments. Obviously killing the woman was not an option since we had no notion of what her powers could become. On the other hand, leaving her with the full capacity to cause further problems for our cause was also not advisable.

I turned to the woman. "You say you are the avatar of another great army in the beyond? You say that you are recruiting others for the purpose of fighting some grand war? Fine. Then I hereby place you under arrest for treason against the United States (not to mention the human race). Lewis! Place her in custody."

Lewis slid the chair out of the way and advanced. The crone retreated back a few steps while looking left and right for a means of escape. Before Lewis could grab her, she scrambled over her table and darted past both of us, knocking her crystal ball off of the table to shatter against the floor. By the time Lewis and I managed to react, she had smashed through her front window and scampered out into the street. Apparently disoriented by the bright sunshine, she veered in a wide circle in the village square.

"She's about to get away, sir," said Lewis, as we both made our way through the shattered debris of the window.

"No, she isn't." I raised my pistol and made full use of my skills as a marksman to fire directly into her leg. In a spray of blood and shattered bone fragments, her right leg collapsed beneath her and she settled to the ground in a bloody heap. As she began to writhe helplessly in agony, I was almost moved to pity.

"Lieutenant," said I, holstering my weapon. "Ensure that she gets the best possible medical care, and that she is treated well. Instruct one of the units to burn her shop to the ground."

I am sorry to say, General, that mine was an imperfect solution. Fortunately for us, Madame Darque will be immobilized for the rest of her life. How long that will be, I cannot say. We must vigilantly retain her as long as possible in a state between life and death to ensure that she cannot use her powers in either.

All I know is that I'm not as comforted when the chaplains tell me of a better place after this one. I'm not as enthusiastically courageous about going to that distant shore in the service of my country as I once was. More importantly, I'm afraid of who might be waiting there for me when I do.

Sincerely,
General Peppenhorst

Representative Sample

Dear Distribution Warehouse Manager:

Please deliver 150kg of *Juggs* magazine to the address specified on the enclosed purchase order. I'm not concerned with the specific content of the issues, although the raunchier they are, the better. Please send your most depraved and sociopathic staff member back into the warehouse to retrieve the magazines for me.

Believe me: you don't want to know why I need them.

Sincerely,
Salvador Narcisse

Dear Mister Manson:

As an executive with Warbling Wind Record Company LLC, I have bemoaned the lack of creative or groundbreaking folk music in our current generation. Nowadays, it seems any person with a beard and an acoustic guitar feels he has the homespun soul required to move an audience of millions.

On the other hand, you are a man who truly understands the nature of human darkness and the call of the blues. I understand you had limited success in locating an agent before the unpleasantness in the late sixties. I do not condone your actions at that time, certainly, but I am compelled as a purveyor of fine music to locate genius wherever it exists. Perhaps your music can vindicate you to the ages.

Please remit one (1) stirring folk ballad of your own creation in the enclosed self-addressed, stamped envelope. I will personally review the content of the work and make preparations for your first CD.

Thank you very much.

Yours,
Salvador Narcisse

Dear Madame Heatherly:

I have been a fervent admirer of your series of books from the very first, *Chitchats with the Overmind*. I find the notion of an all-embracing heavenly force guiding my every move very comforting in a life that (let's face it) simply isn't worth living anymore.

I've discovered that when I release any notion of ambition, hope, or usefulness to the Holy Light, everything feels better. I've even managed to curb my alcoholism and child abuse to one whiskey sour and one piercing glare toward my teenage son a day.

Your books literally changed my life. Please send 150kg of them to the address below using the enclosed American Express purchase order to cover the cost.

Yours in shimmering light,
Salvador Narcisse

Dear Managing Editor:

My mother befell an accident two months ago and during her convalescence has found solace in only one source: your newspapers. The articles keep her informed about the latest trends in such topical subjects as teleportation, spontaneous combustion, and astrology.

Her recovery would significantly accelerate if approximately 150kg worth of issues of your newspaper arrived at her home address listed on the enclosed purchase order. Of particular interest to her open mind are stories about the Bloodsucking Goat Boy, alien abductions, or Lady Diana's desperate efforts to reveal her killer through telepathic contact with the housewives of America.

Thank you in advance for saving my mother's life.

Sincerely,
Salvador Narcisse

Dear Ms. Rumpley:

I'm so glad I found you! After months of research, I was relieved to discover your name in the alumni directory. I am also a Princeton graduate and a friend of Hugh Merton, who I'm sure you remember.

After Hugh's years of public service, no one has written a serious biography of a man who historians specializing in the twenty-first century will consider a seminal influence on American culture.

And you kissed him!

I'm sure you've saved some of his letters throughout the years, and I was wondering if you would be willing to loan those to me as I write his biography. Naturally, I will consider the letters as fragile artifacts and will take care of them accordingly. I am also willing to pay $40,000 for their use for the next thirty days.

Please send as much as you have (preferably close to 50kg) to the address specified on my enclosed business card.

Thank you for helping a scholar immortalize your influence on one of the greatest political figures of our time.

Sincerely,

Dr. Salvador Narcisse,

Professor of American Studies

Dear Dr. Cox:

What a pleasure to make your acquaintance! Why, just last night, Johnny Fincher and I were tipping back a few martinis in the gentlemen's lounge at the alumni club when we discovered we'd both taken your class during our tenure at the university: I in your survey-level astronomy class, and Johnny in a spectrum of classes for his major. What a coincidence!

Of course, the infamous incident of that dreadful paper about Doppler motion he handed in his freshman year came up, and I thought it might be funny after all these years to read it, especially since Johnny has gone on to such a colorful career. I was wondering if you still had a copy and if you'd be willing to forward it to us for a laugh.

I'd be much obliged if you did. I'm considering where to send several of my yearly university donations, and I've been thinking I owe your department a debt of gratitude.

Yours,

Salvador Narcisse

To: Garret Hugh Merton,
  President of the United States of America
CC: Doctor Jonathan Fincher,
  Director of the National Institute of Science

Dear Gentlemen:

I was more sorry than you'll ever know to hear about the premature end to NASA's return to the moon.

My associates (unaccustomed to the industry into which we have recently diversified) take a dim view of business partners who renege on contracts. After your recent withdrawal from our arrangement, it took days of heated discussions to dissuade them from their usual barbaric methods to do something more subtle and agreeable to all.

When you canceled the project for the International Moonbase Project last year, our facilities were on the verge of launching a usable vehicle to deliver the first payloads of materials to the proposed site in the Sinus Aestuum. Unfortunately, you chose at this critical juncture to—as you said in your speech—"focus on the pressing needs of people on Earth."

My employees and investors (not to mention the starving spirits of the entire human race) were left gasping in anticipation for a payoff that never came. More importantly, my associates and I were left with a spacecraft capable of inter-lunar flight but lacking the cargo module we'd originally planned for later this year.

To make the best of an unfortunate situation, we chose to remove the cockpit of the craft, freeing some 500kg of cargo space that we could safely deliver via remote control to the moon.

Our friends in the Russian space agency were happy to accommodate us for our launch, complete with the requisite feelings of bitter irony.

The only question was what to send.

The obvious choices were items representative of our culture as a whole and of you gentlemen in particular. Hence, the cargo manifest of the "American Legacy" was as follows:

— 150kg of tattered, stained issues of *Juggs* magazines from a particularly nasty run in the 70s, labeled "American Art."

— 150kg of dreamy books about spiritualism, tied in neat white ribbons and scented with myrrh, labeled "American Philosophy."

— 150kg of *The Cosmos* newspaper, focusing mainly around an investigative series about Nixon's brain secretly running the National Security Agency and labeled, "American Belles Lettres."

— One sheet of notebook paper containing a poorly-rhymed song called "Puppy Dogs Crying in the Bottom of an Oil Drum," written by Charles Mansion and labeled, "America's National Anthem."

— 50kg of materials duplicated from the private collection of Missy Rumpley (who knew the president during the crest of his collegiate hormones), including letters, sex toys, and three video tapes recorded during spring break involving a hotel room, nylons, and the song, "My Way."

— One college paper written by Doctor Fincher and copied word for word from a graduate thesis written ten years before.

We felt these items were of importance to both the evolving human species and to alien intelligences, either of which will probably encounter them and base their assumptions about our nation (and about you personally) on what they find embedded in the moondust at an undisclosed location on the lunar surface.

Unless, of course, we go up there to retrieve them.

I am confident you will justify our investment in this launch. Feel free to contact me using the enclosed business card if you wish to continue our profitable relationship.

> Looking forward to hearing from you,
> Salvador Narcisse
> CEO, Space Transport Solutions, Ltd.

Bingo

It's disconcerting to come home from a long night working behind the bar at Chili's to find a 100-pound German Shepherd waiting for you.

Worse, a 100-pound *narc* German Shepherd.

"Dude," I said, backing away as the enormous dog bounded to greet me. "What the hell is that?"

"I know what you're thinking, Neil, and yes—it's a dog." Mac rose from his easy chair and held up his hands. "Listen to this. I got the coolest idea from the Discovery Channel." Mac, out of work, spent his days receiving the equivalent of a PhD watching cable documentaries. He knew more about ocelot mating habits than any non-ocelot should know.

"On one of those forensics shows, they had these narc dogs the cops have at the airport sniffing out luggage and looking for coke. They walk around and sniff out dope a machine can't even find. They're like 99% effective."

The dog knocked over our collection of foreign beer cans with a single swoosh of his tail at 100% effectiveness. They rattled to the floor and he backed away to evade responsibility.

"I thought it'd be cool to adopt a retired one, but the cops don't let people like you and me take home a police dog. You've got to be stable and responsible and all."

I didn't like where this was going.

"I pretty much gave up on it until this morning when—like some kind of omen—I get a call from Gina all crying and hysterical. She's leaving Brian and moving back in with my folks."

"Your sister's getting divorced? I'm sorry."

He waved it off. "Yeah, I'm sure she'll be fine. But here's the kicker: two months ago, she and Brian adopted—wait for it—a retired police dog! He doesn't want it, and Mom can't have dogs in the condo. So I said we'd take him."

The dog burrowed his muzzle under a couch cushion, sniffing for contraband. He pulled away in revulsion after a few whiffs, which is what most of us do.

I rubbed my temples and closed my eyes. "Do I even want to ask why you want a police dog?"

He grinned. "It's a stroke of genius. Ever since Julian got busted we've been out a supplier for good weed, right? And we know people living in this building have a taste for the occasional toke, right? I mean, we're across the street from the English department building: every one of them has a stash. All we do is get this dog to find it for us. We send him out sniffing, and liberate what he finds."

"You mean steal it?"

The shepherd trundled over to Mac and rubbed against his leg.

"Is anyone going to tell the cops that someone stole their weed?" He patted the dog with increasing strength. The dog didn't notice until Mac all but pounded him on the back like a lost relative at a wedding. "This hound is our source. We don't need to buy stash ever again!"

"How are we going to get what the dog finds?"

"The Key."

Mac could have been an engineer if he'd ever mustered the strength to lift the cover of a book. He spent his lazy weekday afternoons tinkering with things until he got bored with them. That's why our television, stereo, refrigerator, and other appliances barely worked.

One project Mac did complete was to fashion a master key for the building. We crashed a party at the upstairs apartment of this aerobics instructor Mac hoped to ask out for a date. Once everyone got drunk (but not drunk enough to go out with Mac, alas), he fetched a few keys from the coats hanging in the hallway and laid them out on the kitchen table. He compared them for common features and made a master in the machine shop where he worked that week.

As scary as it sounds to hear a disaffected twenty-year-old pot fiend had access to every apartment in the building, it wasn't bad. Mac was too lazy to steal anything big, and the worst you'd discover would be some coins missing from the laundry kitty or a pillow out of place.

"There are some flaws to your plan, Mac."

"How you figure?"

"Even if the dog will find the goods, you have no idea what kind they'll be. Dogs don't specialize in marijuana. He'll to bring a plastic baggie full of crack rocks with a dealer toting his 9mm close behind. Then what do you do?"

"Easy. Trade in with someone."

"And get shot for your trouble? Or arrested? There's another eight months on the lease of this hellhole, and you can't pay your share from the county lockup." The dog clamped his teeth around my shoe. I tugged, but he growled and held his grip. I jerked my foot away and he skulked into the kitchen. "Besides, what happens when you get the marijuana home and he keeps digging through your stuff to get it again and again?"

"Man, what is it with you? Always going on about how something *can't* be done. You ever try to see if something *can*?"

The animal in question pawed through some dirty laundry and fashioned a lair in the corner of what would be the dining room if we ever dined around a table with napkins and utensils.

I sighed. "What's his name?"

"Gina called him Bingo but that's stupid. I'm going to call him Mellow."

The dog and I exchanged a look and agreed I'd continue to call him Bingo. I sighed. "Well, Bingo, let's get this over with. Come on."

He trotted toward me.

"What are you doing?" Mac blocked the door.

"I'm going to take him to find your drugs."

"Don't be stupid, man. The neighbors would see right through that. We can't send him out for at least a couple weeks, long enough for them to think he's just a normal dog. Besides, they're all home now."

Bingo rubbed his back along the dining room wall and left a streak of dirt.

A couple of weeks?

"He can't live here! He's supposed to be out baying across the British moors, not drinking out of our toilet and sleeping on a bunch of old newspapers. I'm taking him to the pound first thing in the morning."

His eyes widened. "They'll put him to sleep."

"Okay, then I'll drop him off at Petsmart. They have people out front adopting animals on the weekends. I'll just make a deposit instead of a withdrawal."

Mac folded his arms. "Dude, when did you get to be so narrow-minded?"

"Right around the time I got within a few credits of graduating and getting the hell out of here. When I'm gone, you can have Bingo stay with you then. I'm sure he can contribute more to the rent than you do."

I stalked past them both to my bedroom and slammed the door behind me.

It must have been the rhythmic thump of Bingo's hind leg scratching behind his ear that brought Old Man Carroway pounding on our door.

Our downstairs neighbor had retired from some miserable city government office where he denied license, tag, and marriage applications for thirty years. Old habits were hard to break; he was the kind of old man who tells you to quiet down during a good party or yells at kids playing in the street on Christmas morning.

Between episodes of M.A.S.H., he liked to jab a broom handle at his ceiling to tell us to "knock off the damned noise," even though we could never quite identify what he was talking about.

"He's going to turn us in!" Mac bolted from the couch. "Help me get Mellow into the bathroom."

I set down my Calculus book and notepad. "Come on, dog!" I slapped my hand against my thigh and Bingo scuttled over. We shoved him into the bathroom and he leaped into the tub.

"Here's hoping Carroway doesn't have to take a leak."

"Who is it?" I shouted over the banging.

"You know damned well who it is. Carroway. From downstairs."

"I'm sorry, sir," I said, pulling the door open. "I didn't hear you."

Carroway thrust his jowly gray-stubbled face into the apartment and looked around. "What is that scratching noise?"

"Scratching?"

"Right over our bedroom. I keep hearing these snuffling and sucking and scratching noises."

Mac clenched his teeth so he wouldn't laugh.

Carroway shoved past me and into our dining room. He pointed to Bingo's corner. "Something's been digging down toward my apartment."

We leaned over the scratches on the floorboards. Mac stroked his chin for the best appearance of pensive consideration. "Rats?"

"Not in this building, mister. They set traps just two months ago."

"Maybe they're trying to get out."

Carroway put his hands on his hips. "Are we playing games here?"

Mac and I looked at each other. "No, sir."

"I'm not here to play games. I fought in two wars, for Christ's sake. Now where is the dog?"

"What dog?"

"Or cat or ferret or whatever the hell you kids keep in here. Where is it?"

"We don't have any pets, sir."

"They're not allowed above the first floor, you know."

"That's why we don't have one." Mac smiled. "And how are Mrs. Carroway's poodles?"

The man turned to stone before us. His jaw tightened, his fists clenched, his gazed locked on Mac like the tail gunner on a World War Two bomber.

Slowly, he said, "Mrs. Carroway and her poodles have been out of town for the last few days."

So that was it. The brake on Carroway's downhill ride into total misanthropy had been released. She had probably been on the brink of suicide after fifty-odd years of living with a man who thought the Salvation Army should have an assassination squad.

He must have been lonely down there, eating Beefaroni from the can and shouting at the Capitol Gang. We were his only companions, banging around upstairs like the children he'd never had. Would it hurt to be friendlier to him? To invite him over for coffee? I opened my mouth to speak, but he cut me off.

"I'll tell you this, wise guy: we can play games if that's what you want, but you need to know I always win. I'm watching you, and as soon as I see one residence agreement violation, I'm turning you in."

"We just have a few months left in the semester. We can—"

He scowled. "One more violation. One oversized package left in the mailroom. One loud party. One extra car taking up a space not assigned to you." He nodded. "One pet scratching its way into my apartment."

"Yes, sir," I said.

"Out on the street, the both of you."

"Yes, sir," Mac said.

Carroway stepped back into the hall but stopped and turned. "I've seen thirty years of college kids come and go from this building. I've outlasted them all. I'll outlast you, too."

Even through the passenger window encrusted with dog snot, I could see there wasn't anybody offering dogs for adoption outside of Petsmart the next morning.

"Stay here, dog." I cracked open the window for him and locked the doors before I went inside.

A teenager in the fish department was the only available employee, and he wasn't too helpful.

"Adoptions?" he asked, dipping a net into the neons.

"Yeah. Those people you have out front on the weekends, taking applications for dogs and cats."

"Oh! The ASPCA volunteers."

"Yes." Progress. "When are they coming back?"

"The last Sunday of every month. Why? You need a dog?"

"Good God, no. I need to give one back."

The kid frowned and descended the step stool. "They don't take returns."

"He's not a return. He's not defective. He's just not...appropriate."

"Well, you can check the bulletin board for a no-kill shelter, but it isn't cool to abandon a dog."

"I'm not abandoning the dog. I'm trying to find him a better home. Listen—"

A middle-aged lady tugged on the kid's sleeve. "Excuse me, young man."

"Ma'am?"

I had become invisible.

"I thought I should tell someone. I saw a big German Shepherd eating the headrest in a Tercel parked out front. You might want to get on the loudspeaker and warn the owner."

"I'm the owner, lady," I said. "It's my Tercel."

"Your dog looked hungry. Are you here for some chow?"

How do you tell someone you're trying to foist off a dog on Petsmart?

"Among other things."

"A new dog owner, then!" The lady waddled toward me. "How very lucky for you both! You'll need to buy him a dog basket. He needs a place to sleep that's all his own."

Our whole apartment was a giant dog basket, but I picked one out to humor her.

"You'll need a bigger basket. Don't forget some rawhide bones, too." She handed me a huge white bone from the shin of a tyrannosaurus.

"Before I got Echo, my only friends were on *ER*. Now that we walk in the park, everything's different. You've got to make your dog happy so he can do the same for you."

My dog was happy tackling dope dealers and tearing plastic bags of cocaine into a powdery explosion at the airport baggage terminal. I doubted he'd be content chasing birds around the greenway.

"And never buy your dog food from any place other than a pet store. They just sell bags of ash and dung at supermarkets and call it dog chow. It's horrible. Here." She pointed to the most expensive sack on the bottom shelf, fifty pounds of kibble so pricey it might as well have been diamonds.

I hefted the bag into my cart and tried to calculate the available balance on my MasterCard.

"It takes someone special to love a dog, someone with a parental instinct and a big heart. I can tell you've got those."

I was beginning to realize Bingo wasn't just a wall decoration or a new video game. Mac might as well have adopted a child. I guess Bingo's saving grace was that we wouldn't have to buy him a car when he turned sixteen.

"Well, ma'am, thank you for your help. I think this will get us started."

"I hope you have good running shoes. You'll need some traction to stop him."

I smiled and steered my cart to the registers. Fear gripped me: was I ready to own a dog? Or was he ready to own me?

It's just for a month, I said to myself. Then the dog goes to the ASPCA and everything goes back to normal.

When I returned to the car carrying Bingo's temporary possessions, he had already clawed through the seat for a greasy hamburger wrapper (courtesy of Mac, no doubt) and curled up in the back seat to sleep it off.

I dumped the sacks of food in the trunk and slammed it closed. He looked up at me and then settled his head on his paw.

"Don't get too comfortable, pal." Parental instinct or not, the last thing I needed was a son who licked his own testicles.

Bingo turned out to be a better roommate than Mac. He left me alone when I was studying. He put the toilet seat back down after he finished drinking. He never asked to borrow my money or car keys or Moby CDs. He had cleaner feet and fresher breath, too.

I'm not sure we were good roommates for him in return. I was often out at my summer semester class or work, and I found myself worrying about Bingo. Had anyone fed him, or was he licking Doritos dust from Mac's fingers while he slept? Was he trying to hold his urine because no one would walk him? Was he lonely, staring out smudged windows at passersby?

One morning on my way out the door, I almost stepped in a paper plate of mustard. Clutching my uniform shirt, I went to the back bedroom and kicked Mac's food-stained mattress until he opened his eyes and groaned.

"Hey, man, you can't just feed the dog mustard all the time."

"Mustard?" Mac rubbed his eyes.

"He's a carnivore! You can't feed a 100-pound dog condiments."

"He's eaten just about everything else. He's a garbage compactor. The only way we'd get a return on our investment now is if he could detect booze and chicks, too."

Mac's plan to wait awhile and let the dog blend in notwithstanding, there was little hope for anyone thinking Bingo was a "normal dog."

Some poor girl got the shock of her life when Bingo tried to scurry past her onto the second floor. I grabbed him before he made much progress; Carroway lived down there, and the last thing I wanted was an encounter between them. I'm not sure what she had to hide, but she ran trembling past us down the emergency stairwell I used to smuggle Bingo downstairs.

The garbage men didn't like us, either. Bingo seemed fascinated with the row of trash cans behind the building, and barked insanely at the men as they dumped them into the truck when I walked him on Thursday mornings. I shuddered to think of all the packets and bottles and syringes rattling around inside there from our drug-addled neighbors. I'd steer him back toward Franklin Street, out of sight of Carroway's window, before he could make too much noise.

The men tossed the cans back into the alley and clamored back aboard the truck, in a hurry to get away. The driver always clenched his hands around the wheel, and once even gathered the courage to shout as he drove on to the next block, "Get that dog out in the country! He doesn't belong in an apartment!"

Bingo growled as the truck rolled by, and I wondered if those guys were above picking through the trash for my neighbor's "leftovers."

"Sorry, sir!" I yelled after him. "He's harmless." To people who have nothing to hide, I thought. Maybe there were fewer people like that than I knew.

It's funny how your habits change. I used to enjoy just coming home and watching television, but the more Bingo and I walked together outside, the more I enjoyed it. It was nice to listen to your own thoughts and follow Bingo while he explored the streets.

We were out exploring one evening when a gang of tricyclists rounded the corner, red safety flags waving.

The older people in our neighborhood enjoy patrolling the streets on huge tricycles. With their sweaters and baseball caps, they look like benevolent street hoods, not boosting cars but picking up bottles like some sort of Heck's Angels.

I wasn't paying attention while reaching into the mailbox for a student loan check and holding Bingo's leash between two fingers.

That's how he snapped away from me.

"Bingo!" I screamed after him as he scampered down the street, barking away.

They almost escaped. The man on the lead tricycle caught a glimpse of the demon beast pursuing him to the gates of Hell and waved the others on. Pumping their feet like runaway steam engines, they steered the trikes in different directions.

Bingo bore down on the closest just as she veered toward a mound of garbage bags. One caught on the right pedal and ripped open. Bingo leaped over the clattering cans and into the tricycle's rear cargo basket.

The woman screamed.

I wasn't far behind Bingo so I managed to pull him away before he could clamp his jaws down on her neck and worry her like an old sock.

I recognized the trademark knit sweater and shouted, "Everything's okay, Mrs. Carroway! No need to panic!"

The woman turned, her eyes bulging from her skull as Bingo's teeth clicked together hollowly. It wasn't Mrs. Carroway. The sweater looked like hers, but then many older women wear similar clothes.

"Oh, I'm sorry, ma'am. I thought Mrs. Carroway had…"

The man in the lead pedaled toward the scene, and I recognized the scowl immediately. Bingo squirmed and I was tempted to let him go, but the old coot would sue if he survived.

"So this must be the rat scratching his way to my apartment," said Carroway.

He had me, but maybe there was some mercy in his heart. "I know we're not supposed to have dogs in the building, but Bingo here lost his owners and we had to take him in. He'll be out of here in a week or so, I promise."

A smile peeled away from Carroway's grayed teeth. "He will indeed, young man. And you with him."

"That's not necessary, is it?"

Carroway turned to his tricycle harem. "We think it is. We're filing a petition for your eviction first thing in the morning."

"Tomorrow's the Fourth of July."

"Then first thing Monday morning. I guess you have two extra days to choose a bridge overpass for your new home."

Carroway and his entourage pedaled away toward the duck pond. He looked over his shoulder to glower at us just as they crested the hill.

I stooped and scratched Bingo behind the ears.

"Boy, you can't just chase everybody to ground. They're not all drug runners and street hoods." I considered. "Just Mac."

The dog leaned against me, knocking me off balance to the ground. He pressed his head near my face and I patted him.

"You've got to steer clear of some people."

Two weeks ago, the easiest excuse to get rid of Bingo would be for the landlord to have him taken away. That would solve the problem of an enormous dog tearing through our home and eating our scraps and knocking over our garbage.

Now I wasn't sure Bingo was the one I wanted taken away.

I explained the situation to Mac when I got home.

"We've got to do something. Bingo almost ate an old woman today."

He thought about it. "Maybe she's using weed for glaucoma."

"I've got to ask you, Mac: did Gina tell you what kind of police dog this was?"

"What am I, a dogologist?"

"Maybe he's not a drug dog. Maybe he's meant to be chasing down criminals and we're not giving him enough to do."

"Yeah, like in all those cop movies where the cop retires and then has to take one last case because he doesn't know what to do with his life anymore?"

I sighed. "Yeah, just like that. We've got to do something with him. He's bored out of his mind."

"I'll tell you what it is." Mac pointed toward Bingo's nest of torn socks and towels. "The dog's gone crazy. His partner was shot in a gun battle with Colombian drug lords and Bingo watched him die flailing in his own blood. That kind of thing warps a dog, especially a goody-four-paws like Bingo here. He wants revenge. He's just waiting for an opportunity."

"You're an idiot," I said.

"Maybe they had to retire him." Mac's tone was ominous. "He jumps up one of those package ramps, finds a suitcase, rips it open. Turns out it's full of LSD. The dog licks away like crazy and starts tripping out, barking at imaginary fairies, taking nips at the cops because now they look like monsters. They say you never get over an acid trip. Maybe the dog's lost his mind."

Bingo looked up at me and all but rolled his eyes.

"The dog has lost his mind? The dog?" My voice cracked. "You brought him to live here in this tiny filthy apartment to score free pot. You feed him scraps, yell at him, and think he's the one who lost his mind?" I ran my shaking hand through my hair. "Mac, I'd be digging through your stuff, too, just to clean it."

"What's up with you and him, anyway?"

"Nothing. We just bonded because we're the only civilized creatures in this apartment."

"You've sure taken a shine to him—always going out, running around the block and all. You were the one who wanted to get rid of him, remember?"

"And you were the one who got him in the first place."

"Relax, man." He pressed the channel button on the remote and changed to Junkyard Wars. "I'm just saying."

"Just saying what?"

"Forget it, Neil. Never mind."

"No, tell me."

"You're all wound up. Responsible. Ever since we got this dog and you've been taking care of him, you're an adult. You used to be cool, dude. Good for a drink or a smoke or whatever."

"I'm still cool."

"Okay. If you say so." Mac changed the channel again.

"I am." At least Bingo thought so.

"Sure. Of course." Mac changed the channel again. "Look, if you think he's bored, we can just put him to work this weekend. Everybody's going to be away with their folks or at the fireworks, so this is as good a time as any. We'll take him around, get the stuff, and then you can take him to the pound or whatever."

Bingo was no longer the one I wanted to take to the pound.

Maybe there were worse things than eviction—things like living with a roommate who always paid the rent late and didn't take out the trash. I'd gotten older and Mac hadn't; maybe I was aging in dog years with Bingo.

I once hoped a big score would be enough so we could send Bingo away. Now I hoped it would send Mac away instead.

I couldn't afford this apartment by myself, but there were others in the city, big studios with room to run around and maybe a yard downstairs where you could dig.

Might as well put that pet deposit I'd saved to good use.

The next evening after everyone was watching fireworks or away for the weekend, we began our search.

Or tried to: Bingo just sat beside Mac, panting.

"Go on, boy!" I said.

He didn't do anything.

"Maybe there's a command." Mac squatted beside him. "Get drugs!"

No reaction.

"Go pot! Find stash! Get the goods! Gimme the stuff!"

Bingo scratched his ear.

"He's a government dog," said Mac, hitting himself on the forehead with his palm. "Procure illegal substances!"

Bingo looked at us with an expression two or three IQ points below disdain.

I patted my thighs and at least got him to stand up. When I said, "Come on, boy!" and stepped into the hall, he bounded after me.

"We have to go with him."

We led Bingo upstairs from floor to floor. Bingo lifted his head high, turning it from side to side like a weather vane, sniffing in all directions. Once we reached the top floor, he turned around and descended again.

"That's it?" Mac shook his head. "That can't be. I know for a fact these girls have at least a few rolled cigarettes. Bad Bingo! Bad dog!" Mac pointed. "Check again!"

I grabbed Mac's arm while Bingo skulked further downstairs. "If the dog says there isn't anything up here, there isn't anything up here."

"I think the dog is just some kind of idiot or something."

"Funny, he said the same thing about you."

Mac was about to reply when Bingo's constant barking echoed from the second floor.

"He found something!" Mac slapped me on the shoulder. "I knew he could do it."

We found Bingo growling at an all too familiar door.

"Old man Carroway's on the stuff? Dude! Maybe he's lighting up to calm down after being a bastard all day."

Bingo pawed against the door, bulging it inward.

"That can't be," I said. "Maybe it's just prescription medicines."

"I don't think Bingo would react like this for a bunch of old bottles of Lasix."

Mac was right. Bingo, frantic now, tried to burrow underneath.

Mac leaned over and inserted his key.

"Ready?"

I checked my watch. Carroway was probably still on his evening tricycle patrol, so I nodded.

Mac swung the door open. Bingo launched through like a missile and ran for the back of the apartment.

We looked around as he sniffed the baseboards. Carroway kept the house as we expected he would: stacks of old "Limbaugh Letters" on the coffee table, plastic coverings on the couch and chairs, bundles of mail on a tidy desk. The room reeked of sweet perfume, covering the stench of old TV dinner boxes and hair tonic.

Mrs. Carroway's decorative taste ranged from bright orange floral to bright yellow floral with some splashes of purple floral between. A tray of old rings and bracelets Zsa Zsa Gabor would consider too tacky rested on the kitchen table, perhaps on their way to the pawn shop.

Mac shook his head. "Some people have no taste."

I was about to mention his milk crate bookcases when Bingo ran into the bedroom. He tore the sheets and pillows into an exploding spray of feathers and foam.

"Man, he's going to town. Good boy, Bingo!"

Bingo was just about to tear the mattress off the bed when the front door slammed against the wall and Carroway burst inside.

"What is going on here?"

I ran into the bedroom to grab Bingo while Mac turned toward Carroway. "Uh, hello, sir."

"What are you doing in my apartment?" He looked past Mac to check what I was doing.

Mac glanced down. "Nothing, sir. The door was standing open and I'm afraid the dog got loose and ran inside. We got here just in time."

"Just in time for what?"

I pulled Bingo into the living room by the collar as he wriggled to break free.

Mac swallowed. "Just in time for us to lock the door for you before someone broke in."

"It seems someone already has." He craned his neck toward the bedroom. Then, grinning, he picked up his phone and dialed. "Looks like you'll be out of here before Monday after all."

I reached toward him. "Mister Carroway—"

He turned his back to me and spoke into the phone. I couldn't make out the words, but it wasn't hard to figure out who he was calling.

I traded glances with Mac. Some visceral, animal instinct encouraged me to run, to jump into the car and get out of town. That's what Mac would do: hit the road like a character in a Steinbeck novel. I wouldn't be as lucky. They'd kick me out of school and find me wherever I went.

Carroway hung up and folded his arms. "They're on their way."

"You don't have to press charges, you know," said Mac, the amateur attorney. "You can just sign a complaint and it doesn't go on anybody's record. No harm, no foul, right? We weren't stealing anything."

Carroway shook his head. "How do I know that?"

There are few half hours more awkward than standing in someone's apartment waiting for the police to come and haul you away. Mac or I would sometimes try to appeal to his human kindness, but Carroway had long ago purged that from his soul.

"Can we at least go back to our own place?" Mac tried to get us out of the room, at least.

"So you can make a break for it? I don't think so."

"You know where to find us. Can we at least take the dog upstairs?"

Carroway glowered at Bingo. "No, he's staying right here with us."

When the uniformed man arrived, Mac and I were surprised to see he wasn't a police officer.

"I'm from county Animal Control," he said. "We've had reports of a dangerous dog."

Animal control? Why hadn't Carroway called the police? Why take Bingo away when we were the ones who had broken in?

Bingo stood behind me, and the officer unfolded a leash.

"Wait! We'll leave right now. I'll take the dog with me, and we'll just get out."

"Sorry, son." He clasped the leash to Bingo's collar. "Pending an investigation, the animal has to be taken to the county shelter."

Bingo settled to the floor like a sixties protester, sooner dragged from the scene than leaving under his own power. The officer was willing to oblige. He curled his fingers under the collar and tugged Bingo toward the stairs. The dog let out a single yelp and writhed against his grip.

"At least let me take him down. You're hurting him."

Mac and I followed the officer down the steps as Carroway lagged behind. My voice echoed through the building and people opened their doors to look.

"I do this every day, kid," he replied.

We emerged at the ground floor and the officer backed through the steel door, Bingo squirming in his grasp.

We scuttled through the parking lot toward the county truck, and I couldn't let it go any farther. I grabbed for my dog's collar myself, peeling away the officer's fingers. He fought me back, and as we wrestled, Bingo backed through the collar and set himself free.

He ran toward the line of garbage cans, barking hysterically. Carroway made a half-hearted attempt to chase him, but Bingo knocked one over before he could stop him. Kicking up a spray of papers and boxes, Bingo seemed jubilant and in his element, like an artist fulfilling his vision after long years of practice. He yanked at something, wrested it free, and bounded back to me with the goods clamped in his mouth.

Bingo dropped the gray-green severed hand at my feet, orange and purple costume rings still on the fingers. I patted him on the head. He trained me well.

The fascination with digging toward Carroway's apartment. The interest in the trash cans and the second floor. The attraction to Mrs. Carroway's sweater. Bingo knew what Carroway was all along. And now I knew what Bingo was.

A cadaver dog.

Mac whirled away, stooping to the ground and gagging. The animal control officer blanched, clutching at his walkie talkie.

Carroway's eyes frosted and his lips tightened to a slit. He stepped backwards from the scene as our neighbors leaned from their windows and dialed the police on cordless phones.

Bingo growled by my side.

"I wouldn't go any further if I were you, Mister Carroway." I felt like Clint Eastwood, pointing a German Shepherd instead of a .357 Magnum. "This dog has tackled quicker men than you in his day."

Carroway didn't play along by pulling a gun or vowing revenge. He just settled against a car and slid to the ground while we waited for the police.

You'd think catching a murderer in your apartment building would win you some special treatment: a break on the rent, at least, or a waived pet deposit.

We were still evicted, although the manager decided to terminate our lease with no strings attached. I guess he was worried about what else Bingo would find in that dump.

I hear Mac moved in with a fraternity. He's serving as technical advisor to schemes and stunts that make the student newspaper interesting reading again.

Bingo and I testified only briefly at Carroway's trial. Other witnesses and investigators offered more ghoulish details: Mrs. Carroway's severed parts had been distributed among the weekly trash pick-ups, and the sweater she had worn when she died was a gift to a new girlfriend, one with a better personality for Carroway's taste but not quite the right look.

Given the physical evidence, it didn't take the jury long to deliberate, and as Carroway was taken to begin his sentence, I resisted the temptation to tell him his new neighbors would be much worse than we were.

Bingo seems happily retired now. Maybe that last case got the fever for law enforcement out of his system. Still, when we're walking around our new apartment complex and he starts digging in the bushes, I just pull him away and pretend I didn't see anything.

You're Welcome

I'll admit it: I'm a lover of zombie women, a connoisseur of corpses, an aficionado of grayed flesh, twisted teeth, and vacant stares. Nothing turns me on like groaning dead prowling for ripe human brains.

Who could guess this innocent kink would cause the Zombie Renaissance and make me a publishing mogul? I just wanted a dead girl to love me again.

When I met Dixie Elwood, she was a very live fellow sixth-grader and gym class inmate. Taller than everyone else in our class, she was already encumbered with curves beneath her t-shirt that evoked new and embarrassing feelings within my heart, my brain, and... other places.

My friends, also suffering from embarrassing feelings, contented themselves with peering up her shorts in the reflective gym floor, but that wasn't enough for me. Current fashion provided a convenient bell pull of early adolescent desire: a ponytail swishing side to side as we ran our laps. One day in class I just reached forward enough to give it a forceful (yet tender, I thought) tug.

Her head snapped back and her sneakers squeaked to a stop. Then, with a feral glimmer in her eyes, she chased me around the gym in ever-widening circles until she finally tackled me beneath the bleachers and pinned me to the floor.

There, pressing against me, sweat beaded on her upper lip, she grinned and pressed her mouth to mine. Then she shoved off of me and walked away.

So started our ritual of the tug, the chase, and the tumble that continued for the rest of the semester. Once Coach Martin gave up teaching us any kind of physical fitness, we pursued a strict regimen of self-study beneath the bleachers. There, we honed our talents for kissing, evolving over the weeks from a peck to open mouths to the Holy Grail: tongues!

On the day Dixie and I crossed that threshold, we walked home together with satisfied smirks. We'd explored a frontier our classmates only saw in television shows and naughty books smuggled from Dad's dresser. We were Lewis and Clark, ready to conquer a new world.

We weren't paying attention when we crossed the street, and I guess my quick Pop Warner football reflexes saved me from the bus that knocked poor Dixie into the mulberry bushes and subsequently into the province of the dead.

I was too stunned by the shrieking brakes and groaning horn to be there when she died; by the time I got to her, she was already gone. Her eyes gazed straight ahead toward our next kiss, but the paramedics pulled me away before I could give it to her.

I knew I wouldn't be invited to the funeral. I was just another kid in gym class—one who happened to be Dixie's only true love. It seemed so unfair that I knew her better than anyone, but I wouldn't even get to see her again.

Then I got lucky. Because everyone was so devastated at the loss of such a shining light (as the obituary said), Dixie's parents opened the service to "those in the community who loved her." I qualified more than most.

Best of all were two thrilling words: "open casket." I could get a last look at my first love.

Everyone from the neighborhood stretched in a long line in front of the coffin. As each of us shuffled closer, I leaned from side to side to get a look at her. She seemed more beautiful than ever: pearled and waxy like those ceramic statues at Hallmark. Her closed eyes and protruded lips seemed even to anticipate a kiss.

I glanced around.

In front of me, little Jenny Harrington moaned to her family that she'd never see Dixie in Girl Scouts again. Behind me, a few elderly neighbors whispered about how lifelike she seemed.

Now or never.

I leaned in and pressed my lips to Dixie's. The cold rubbery flesh sent a shiver through every nerve. I pressed harder, opened my mouth, and slipped my tongue inside.

The funeral director happened to look over at the casket at just that moment. His gentle smile eroded into a snarl.

Right then—and I'll swear on a stack of my own pornographic magazines—Dixie slipped her tongue back!

I opened my eyes to make sure she was still dead. Her eyes remained closed, and her tongue swished away as the funeral director yanked me back from the coffin.

"What the hell is the matter with you, boy?" he cried.

I couldn't answer. I savored Dixie's flavor in my mouth, a cold balloon filled with flowers.

Mom and Dad weren't too happy about the corpse-kissing thing. They grounded me for three weeks and sent me to Pastor Andersen. We talked about how to handle my grief, but I was more interested in asking him when a soul goes to heaven.

"At the moment of death, I suppose," he replied.

"Are you sure it doesn't, say, wait until after the funeral?"

"I don't think so. Why?"

"Because Dixie couldn't have slipped her tongue in my mouth if she was already with the angels."

He sputtered and stammered and suggested some Bible verses, but none of them helped.

All through my adolescence, I dreamed of Dixie waiting for me in her coffin with that polka-dotted dress, fantasizing about digging her out with Dad's shovel to love her one more time. I wondered how high school would have been if we had still been together.It would have been one hell of a prom, at least.

Boys aren't supposed to think that way, though, so I gave living girls every chance, but normal girls just didn't do it for me. They were too tan, for one thing, and too quick moving for another. Plus, they chattered about a million boring things, all while I waited to get down to business. "Do you like my blouse? What do you want to see at the movies tonight? Come inside and meet my father! Why do you want to watch *Night of the Living Dead* again?" On and on and on. Living girls were too high maintenance.

Dixie would have been easy.

In college I discovered the only possible replacement for Dixie that might be as stiff and gray as my fantasies envisioned her: the Goth community, with their black dresses, pasty skin, and sunken eyes. Mine liked to call herself Raphelia, but her real name was Nicole.

She was great most of the time. She could get frisky in the theater during haunted house flicks, and sometimes she'd groan "Brains!" during our love-making. I got bored playing those depressing role-playing games, though, and we fought a lot.

"You don't understand what darkness means," she told me once during a live-action vampire role-playing session. We were standing outside our haunted manse (an abandoned McDonalds) waiting for other denizens of the night to join us.

"What are you talking about?"

She squished a rubbery breast back into her corset while trying to look disaffected and glum. "You think it's all about death."

"Well, that and sex." I bundled my regulation vampire trench coat around me.

"It's not. It's about recognizing that only after dying to the mundane world do we become alive. We resurrect ourselves, Tom. We rise together in the night."

"Yeah. Sure." She could get on my nerves.

We lived together in an apartment stocked with black candles and witchcraft books. Friends came over on Friday nights with bottles of Sutter Home and bags of weed to watch bad horror movies and squirm in a pale fleshy blob on the beanbag chairs.

We were comfortable in our dreariness. At least I was, anyway.

One night Nicole called out to me from her shower over the rush of the water, so I paused *Day of the Dead* and sauntered into the bathroom.

She stood glistening in the tub, her make-up gone, her tongue stud removed, her hair long and brown. She motioned me to get in with her, so I shucked my clothes and squirmed inside.

She felt warm and alive under the constant rain with me. No pasty make-up. No black dresses. No angst. Just a woman rubbing against me in a shower.

She leaned in and nuzzled my shoulder. "Let's get married."

I stepped back against the tiles. "Married? You said you never wanted to be mundane."

"We won't be." She clasped my hands. "I want to start living. I don't want to skulk in the darkness anymore."

I guess she outgrew her early-twenties malaise.

We made love that night and she was animated and passionate. She fell asleep beside me and I got up, packed a few belongings, and left.

The last thing I need is a woman who wants to live.

There was just no substitute for Dixie. I had to have the real thing, death or no death. I couldn't stand it any longer.

I had to dig her out myself.

In retrospect, my midnight mission into the cemetery to rescue Dixie from the embrace of oblivion wasn't carefully considered. Okay, I was drunk.

It took hours and almost a whole case of beer to dig my way down to Dixie's coffin. When I imagined her waiting in the dark, panting with anticipation, remembering our kisses, squirming in the casket with ghoulish erotic joy, it wasn't like work anymore.

Dixie's coffin was stronger than I remembered. People aren't buried in pine boxes anymore, and these new aluminum lacquer jobs are a bitch to open. Jesus had better bring a can opener on Judgment Day because it's almost impossible to crack those bastards open.

I tried wedging my shovel into the seam but no luck. I tried rolling the coffin on its side so she'd tumble out, but it didn't work. I tried jumping up and down on the lid hoping it would cave in so I could peel one end up, but it never did.

It was probably the jumping and my loud cursing that summoned the night watchman to the grave.

At least he kept his cool. "Excuse me, sir," he said, all polite, leaning over with his lantern. "You got a permit?"

I, sadly, did not keep my cool. "Here's my permit, pal." I shot him the finger and kept slamming the shovel on the lid of the casket.

"I'll call the police!"

"Whatever, man."

It was time to give up anyway. When I tried to crawl out from the hole, though, I kept sliding down the loose soil and back into the grave again.

Fortunately, the police eagerly helped me out.

On my attorney's advice, I declined to take the stand in my own defense. That was a pity, really: I wrote an impassioned plea that it wasn't defiling a grave if you *loved* the person inside it. My attorney's claims of my drunkenness earned me probation and community service.

I learned my lesson, though: you can't just go digging people up without a plan. Next time, I'd be more organized.

I was trapped between two worlds. I wanted the listlessness of the dead, but the activity (not too much!) of the living. I'd tried the cemetery but just couldn't get what I needed. I'd tried the Goth scene and got too much. I was a man who'd never know true sexual satisfaction.

Could Dixie be the only woman in the world for me? Or was she just the best example I'd ever seen of my heart's true desire?

Then it hit me one night during *Creature Feature*: zombies!

That's what Dixie had that no other woman did: powdery skin, black sunken eyes, and—best of all—no issues. No anniversaries. No arguments. No weddings. No tricky questions like "Am I fat?" or "Do I look better than Gwyneth Paltrow?"

I'd sit by Dixie's grave for hours trying to think of how to build a bridge between us. Then I'd go home and color the girls in *Hustler* with a gray crayon.

A motivational speaker on late-night television inspired me to realize dreaming wasn't going to accomplish anything and I had to get down to business. I didn't take his advice and buy the fifty gallon drum of hair cream, but I decided that as soon as I woke up, recovered from my hangover, got the mail, and had some waffles, I would dedicate myself to learning every possible method of raising Dixie from the dead.

They don't have many books at your local library about such subjects. I've looked. Don't bother.

I'd have to do my research on the streets talking to people who knew about zombies, zombification, and the general logistics of, say, digging up an old girlfriend and marrying her. Can she share a bank account with you? Does she need to register somewhere? It's all very confusing.

If one city in America knows about shambling legions of darkness marching in the night, it would be New Orleans. I packed my bags and flew there for a two-week research sabbatical from work. My manager at Kinko's didn't mind.

People are tight-lipped about resurrection in the Big Easy. Apparently the Chamber of Commerce is fighting the city's reputation as the stomping grounds of freaks and screwballs. That's why it took almost a week to corner some grizzled old man in a convenience store playing checkers who gave me my only decent lead, directions to a store run by a seventh-generation shaman with an eye toward necromancy.

I expected to find this guy in a shanty at the end of some winding street, but he ran a pet store in the mall. As mall stores go, it was shady and sinister, I'll admit, but the people buying huge rawhide bones shattered the ambiance.

After the last customer left and the shaman had validated his parking pass, I asked him the question that had burned in me for almost twenty years.

"Got anything for raising the dead?"

He looked around to be sure the store was empty. "How big?" he asked impatiently. "I got nothing for dogs. Only cats and rabbits, today."

"You resurrect dead pets?"

He scowled. "This a pet shop, no? Parents come with hamsters in little bags and beg me for one just like it so the kid don't know." He sighed. "The kid *always* knows. It just be easier to reverse entropy than to deal with a surly child. You learn when you have kids."

No fear of that for me. "How does it work?"

"How would I know? You ask your mama how biscuits rise? Maybe cats do the same thing. Thing is, I use a potion instead of yeast."

"Are the animals… different?"

"Different? Different how?"

I had to ask. "You know. Evil or something?" It would suck if Dixie returned from the dead just to slit my throat in my sleep. I could get a living girl to do that.

He shook his head. "How could I tell? The fuckers get back in their wheels and start running again. They don't cackle or rub their paws together, if that what you asking."

Perfect.

"What kind of animal you need raised?" he asked.

"Does it matter?"

"Well, the recipe proportions are different."

I tried to calculate Dixie's mass in pets so I could multiply the recipe. Two German Shepherds? Fifteen cats? Sixty hamsters?

I took a chance. "She's a Maine Coon cat." I figured Dixie would be about ten Maine Coon cats and I could just multiply the recipe by the easiest number possible.

"Okay. I've got what you need." He reached under the counter and then paused. "You not gonna raise a person from the dead, are you?"

I opened my mouth in surprise. "Good God, no. That'd be sick!"

"Because if you are, you better think twice. This stuff do strange things to people. They ban it back on the islands."

I swallowed. "No, sir. Just a cat."

He handed me a brown jar.

"The instructions are inside. I've included a few of the less common components you have to fly to Haiti to get your hands on. Everything else you buy in the stores."

He rang up my purchase on the register and told me the steep price I'd expected. I handed him the last wad of bills from my savings account, reminding myself the money wasn't as important as Dixie.

"Remember: a little go a long way."

"Right."

"And if there any left over, don't just dump it down the sink."

"Got it."

I paused for a moment. He thrust out his hand and I rested my parking pass in it. He punched the validation and then turned back to his battered books.

It took awhile to gather the materials (and to answer some pointed questions at Home Depot). I loaded the barrels into a rented truck and drove to Dixie's cemetery. This time, I read through the funeral announcements in the paper and discovered when the caretaker would be busy with another burial so I could roll out the cart of materials without anyone noticing.

They had done a good job of covering her grave with new sod. You couldn't tell I'd been there the first time.

I measured out ten times the amount of chemicals and it still didn't seem like it would be enough. Looking at the little jar I'd prepared and at all the jugs and cartons I'd bought, I decided to use it all.

I wanted her back fast.

I poured the goop into the grass, and (as a courtesy to the shaman's twisted religion) performed his ceremony. I had trouble with the language, but I got it close enough. Clouds raced across the sky. Thunder rumbled. Lightning sizzled. A green fog oozed over the landscape and the earth cuddled in it like a child on Christmas Eve shivering with anticipation.

I waited. Just when I turned to go back to Home Depot for more chemicals to try again, the earth beside her stone stirred. A gray hand with dark fingernails sprouted from the soil like a flower.

I couldn't contain my excitement. I clasped that hand to pull her from her prison, struggling against her heavy earthen blanket to yank her back into the daylight.

As the sod and silt poured away, though, I realized the full horror of my mistake. I'd fantasized for twenty years about her soft zombie moans and lumpy zombie figure, never comprehending a simple truth about death.

You don't grow in the tomb.

Dixie—still thirteen, still wearing her blue polka dotted dress—curled her black lips from her teeth and snapped at me.

She was still beautiful. I could almost have kissed her. But twenty years had gone by. I was a man and she was a child (although a zombie child) and I just couldn't do it. Pedophilia was just too far. We all have our standards.

I'd raised a dependent from the dead, a child I'd have to send to school and pick up from cheerleading practice, a child who would never grow into the woman I needed to make me whole.

There was one thing to do. I ran back to the rental truck as she followed, clawing the air. I rummaged behind the seat among the safety equipment and wrested a jack handle from the emergency kit.

Just as she extended her claws, I swung the steel bar, tearing into her loose flesh. I pounded again and again until she crumbled into a dozen rotting chunks of flesh.

Weeping and exhausted, I fell to the ground and held my head in my hands. I'd killed my one true love twice and she could never come back again.

Unfortunately, the slamming of tombstones against the ground and the creaking of tomb doors interrupted my pageant of self-pity. Gray bodies scratched from the soil, faces leering in gleeful anticipation, teeth sparkling in the light. They staggered closer, groaning and growling and gnashing their teeth.

I looked down to see more of the fluid gurgling into the earth. I'd done a lot more than kill Dixie, it seemed.

I stumbled backwards toward my car and tried to think of what to do next. I couldn't fend all of them off, and at that moment the prospect of letting them tear me into pieces wasn't altogether uninviting.

Just as I was about to surrender to their final clammy embrace, I saw—far in the back—the woman who would change my life. Still wearing the long red dress and black veil in which she'd been buried, her jaw lolled toward the side of her skull and a patch of maggots surged on her sexy neck.

It wasn't Dixie I wanted. It was rot. It was entropy. It was the path of least resistance.

My fear and despair dissolved as I fell in love with the woman who would become my wife and the world's first dead centerfold. I discovered my calling: to introduce the beauty of the dead to the living.

She wasn't easy to capture, and I have the scars to prove it. Still, that stunning corpse, known now as Evelyn, was one of the two greatest factors in my rise as a millionaire and a popular celebrity. The other, of course, was the seeping of my chemical brew into Chicago's water table resulting in a new minority culture, one capable of spreading by bite and claw.

My work was simple. I just chronicled it and photographed the gorgeous women for everyone to enjoy. The money rolled in from people fascinated by the newest sexual adventure.

I started with a website, www.sexcarcass.com, that surged in popularity as the zombies spread across America. We outgrew our servers several times, and by the time our electronic infrastructure went down in the short-sighted war, I'd already decided to start publishing a magazine.

Soon *Playghoul* was in every convenience store, truck stop, and horror convention dealers' room in America. Our first print run was gone in six days and bootleg copies of our books appeared in every format.

With the money, I bought Dixie a new tomb where I could visit, but as time went on, I stopped by less and less often. She was just a symbol of something else I needed.

That something else lived with me at my new mansion in the Colorado mountains, enjoying the local wildlife, scenery, and brains. I don't like them as much as Evelyn does yet, but I'm developing a taste.

Best of all, she doesn't mind the eight other women who live with us. No two are alike, and we have a good time. Sometimes I have to let them go out and prowl, but they come back sated and frisky.

Sure, there's been a ten thousand percent increase in brain-eating fatalities in the world. But to me, the grave is half full. While those religious types all cry "Waaah! This is an abomination unto the Lord," I welcome the new pool of fascinating sexual partners for those of us cool enough to enjoy the new world order.

As the last generation of prudes becomes zombies themselves, people ask why I have so many subscribers. Since we pornographers say what everyone else just thinks about in the shower, I'll tell you.

We all want zombies to love us: partners who never complain, never argue, and never leave the toilet seat up or sanitary napkins in the wastebasket. The difference between you and me is that I like mine gray.

I've given the world the perfect romantic fantasy.

You're welcome.

Solidity

Each day you emerge from Metro Center station and discover a chorus line of mumbling bums awaiting you on the street. They shuffle, they mutter, they bark, they shout at nothing.

They shout at nothing.

You walk by, wondering the same thing every day: what the hell are they yelling at? Like any metro passenger, you are a practiced eavesdropper, so sometimes you try to make sense of their crazed conversations with subdimensional beings.

"Frippety frop grap!" cries a man resting on a bench. You can't tell if he's quoting a Disney movie, imitating Bill Cosby, or speaking his own invented language.

A woman with a tattered Redskins hat stares right behind you and says, "Mama never thought she was going to hell until she saw the hooves."

"The crack cocaine's done drove down the price of whore," wails one grizzled gentlemen dressed in plastic grocery bags. You stop, fascinated by his economic treatise. "Time was a man paid top coin for kitty," he says, nodding like Socrates to a circle of newspaper boxes. "Now boy wants happy, he just lights the pipe."

You clutch your briefcase and walk on by.

Every morning in your third floor cubicle you turn on your computer. You call the minutes between the Windows 2000 logo and connecting the last network drive your "thinking time," and you spend them wondering why you're not a famous actor or international spy yet. Lately, you've been pondering bums.

Weren't bums once friendly, happy-go-lucky people? Didn't they do odd jobs and hop the rails singing songs about America's heartland? Wasn't Woody Guthrie a bum? Or was he a hobo? Is there a difference? Maybe a hobo is a bum who rides on trains. What do they call bums who ride on, say, the metro?

You're late for a meeting. Your boss drones on about vertical markets and leveraging thin-client synergy while you consider the larger questions of the universe. Are you seeing an increase in bums waiting for you outside the metro? Is that a function of a slowing economy, a deregulated mental health system, or an ambivalent society marching headlong into psychological entropy?

And who are they talking to?

Someone makes a lame joke about client-server architecture and everyone laughs. "Just give me my goddamn check," you mutter behind the secretary's horsey chortle.

What if vagrants are prophets refusing a call from God? The burning bush appears as some sort of argumentative creature requiring shouting and gesticulating. But then, why would God contact people so incompetent to act on his behalf, people who'd take his holy orders and sleep them off in a Thunderbird-induced stupor?

More importantly, why doesn't he call you?

The gourmet coffee machine in the breakroom is out of Mocha Francais again, and you stalk back to your cubicle and write an angry e-mail demanding to know why. It's such a simple thing, coffee; how hard can it be to keep a full supply?

A glacier of file folders chips away to the floor, but you don't bother to pick them up. You review meeting agendas and approve spreadsheets and write documents you never quite remember. Outlook chimes with another appointment and you click the dismiss button; three more e-mails about scheduled system outages flicker on the screen as you delete them.

You launch PlanView to enter last week's timesheets and wonder if bums punch into some cosmic timeclock and justify every second with some authority. Do they charge time to project GF230, Arguing with Trees? TR761, Stalking Rabid Squirrels in the Park?

As project EE210 scrolls by—Entering Timesheets—you feel envious. Their daily work may be differently worthless than yours, but at least they get to see the stars. Maybe those bums are the evolutionary avatars of new human beings who reject the work-a-day world and live in the province of the mind.

It still doesn't explain who they're talking to.

Since there is no project code for Spinning Theories about Vagrancy, you put all forty hours into project EF590, Administrative Time.

After another day successfully feigning importance, you walk to the station and try not to make eye contact with anyone. A man flings a Styrofoam cup full of what you hope is Mountain Dew at a lamppost while he shouts, "Eat that, bitch!"

The notion enters your mind that these people don't find their invisible companions to be enjoyable at all, that they are stalked by forces from whom they never escape. The lovable imaginary friends who guard us in childhood become imaginary enemies, shedding fur to reveal scales.

"Jesus," you say under your breath. How depressing. The sun sets behind the station and you shudder.

No explanation makes total sense to you, even after working the problem for months. The curiosity burns in you worse than Night Train, and you decide there's no way to solve the problem without getting first-hand evidence. You're going to have to corner a bum and just ask him.

You're afraid to accost the ones at Metro Center. These are journeyman vagrants who have studied the art of filth-encrusted madness until they have achieved its highest art. Were there Nobel Prizes for urban anomie, this gauntlet on G Street would be headed for Stockholm.

Plus, you don't need your supervisor seeing you holding an existential conversation with a lunatic, even if that is what you do all day working for him.

You wait until you get home to King Street. There, the bums are more sedate, more comfortable in their madness. They don't shout at their demons until the sun has gone down and the shadows grow long.

It's just that time when you leave the station. The few commuters who work as late as you do spread to their secondary forms of transit and you're standing near the curb beside a man who will make everything clear. He's even mumbling to himself already. You step closer, leaning to listen.

"Better not make the crows angry anymore," he whispers.

You make the first move. "Hey! Over here!"

The man turns, raising a dirty paw to his mouth.

"I'm not going to hurt you." You hold out your hands to prove it. "Peace, brother."

He takes a step backward anyway.

"I've got to ask you a question."

He whispers into his hand.

"Who the hell are you talking to?"

The man's face spasms like an invisible sculptor is crushing it as clay.

"Look around you. It's just you and me here, buddy. Who are you talking to?"

The man shakes his head like he doesn't understand.

"I'm the only person here who is real." You stamp on the sidewalk. "I'm the only one who is solid."

"As solid as I am," he says, almost too softly to hear.

"What?"

Just then, your spouse drives up to the curb in the Acura.

"What did you say?" You approach the bum again, but he stands his ground.

A shout comes from your car. "You ready to go, babe?"

"Just a minute," you say. "I'm asking this bum a question."

Your spouse pauses. "What bum?"

Exit Laughing

He was just dying out there on that stage.

"If cheese food is supposed to taste like cheese, what is baby food supposed to taste like? Is anyone looking in those giant vats at the Gerber plant?"

A few coughs emerged from the otherwise silent audience.

The comic swallowed nervously. "If Soylent Green was people, did heavy smokers taste like beef jerky?"

A lady sitting near the back spit her drink out into the aisle.

"Why do kids think there are monsters in the closet?" he demanded, melting like a tub of ice cream under those horrible stage lights. "I mean, what's the tactical advantage there? Is there some monster black market for filthy socks, roller skates, or forgotten action figures? Is there some hidden totemic value to the bogeyman of last winter's hockey stick? Man."

From my seat at the bar, I could see the audience squirming on his behalf. Kind-hearted people chuckled; others stared at him in stunned silence. A few shook or tapped their watches, puzzled why time had slowed to a crawl.

The comic ran a quivering hand through his wispy gray hair and continued despite all reason. "Monsters? Ha! Let me tell you, boys and girls" – he jabbed a crooked finger out at the audience – "those monsters ain't in the closet. They're at the Greyhound station. And the Safeway. And the Discount Furniture Warehouse. They're not your lovable bogeyman, either - they're tall, slimy bastards with eye stalks and flippers and one moldy tusk that can crack open a human skull with a single peck and spray the warm, gray oozing goodness all over your best Pierre Cardin suit, baby!"

A woman in the front row shrieked, bolted from her chair, and ran weeping to the exit. Her husband stalked after her and the audience stared at the comedian in mute astonishment.

"They're out there, baby," he yelled after her. "Don't you forget it!" He looked off the stage at a shadow frantically gesticulating to him.

"Well, folks, I guess it's time to go. You've been great. Let's have a hand for the band."

The audience exploded in relieved applause as the man behind the piano smiled sheepishly. The comic staggered from the stage, dropped his microphone in a glass of beer, and limped toward the bar. Everyone gave him a wide berth.

He wasn't a tall man, or a handsome one, or a fat or thin one. He was decidedly average, and I'm not sure if I could point him out to you if I saw him on the street today. Graying hair, middle-aged paunch, weak chin: these were all so ordinary. I might recognize the clothes, because they were rumpled and sweaty. They looked like they'd rubbed an awful lot of bus seats during the night.

He climbed up on the bar stool next to mine and asked the bartender for a screwdriver. He fumbled in his pockets for something but then gave up.

"Tough room," I said, tentatively.

He turned to me and narrowed his eyes. "I've seen worse. Much worse."

"How long have you been doing this?"

"Eighteen months. Before that, I was a lawyer."

I stared at him. "Don't take this the wrong way, mister, but I'm not so sure you should have given up your day job for this."

He hacked out a single-syllable laugh that sounded like a bark. "I didn't want to, believe me. I'm a much better attorney than I am a comic. But I have to."

"Why?"

He slouched down further in his seat and leaned closer to me. "Have you ever faced cosmic evil, buddy?"

"Cosmic evil? I'm not sure."

He held up a hand. "I don't mean hum-drum regular work-a-day evil. I don't mean your typical evil, like murder or rape or extortion. I mean evil so powerful and megalithic that to face it, to admit you've seen its hideous nature, is to crumble the foundations of your beliefs, make your bible a lie, and turn every beautiful aspect of nature into a monument of filth."

I considered for a moment. "I don't think I've faced cosmic evil, then, according to that definition. I take it you have?"

"Oh, yes." He tipped his glass to his lips and belted down a mouthful of liquor. "I've seen the face of the devil. And he looks a lot less like Neil Diamond than you'd think."

"Where did you see that?"

"You don't want to know. The totality of that horror would rot your soul like an Englishman's teeth."

"Come on, now. That just makes me curious."

"You don't want to know."

"Then why would you start telling me the goddamned story?"

He looked up at me. "Look, buddy, I'm just trying to protect you. The truth is uglier than you think. If you want to hear a little bedtime story before we close for the night, something to keep your eyes open and fixated on the ceiling above your bed all night, then I'll oblige. You're not going to like it, but then I've always said comedy ain't pretty."

He blotted sweat from his brow with a yellowed handkerchief and then began his story.

About two years ago, my wife Tricia and I decided to drive to various destinations in the south, mainly in Florida. You know: Disney, Sea World, the beaches, the whole bit. We were in full tourist regalia, ready to capture a fun-filled couple of weeks in America's playground.

We'd just left the Everglades when Trish points out this little town on the map and asks if we can swing through and see some quaint country living with porch rockers and old men in suspenders playing checkers. The little town was in the dead center of the state, and it's one of those places that's nothing more than a crossroads. It's Florida's colon: everything passes through.

Now, it doesn't look evil when you drive through it. They hide it well. They've got just the right number of befuddled hillbillies, just the right filthy convenience stores and barefoot Wal-Mart patrons and rabid dogs chained to pickup truck beds. Nothing to arouse suspicion. Just business as usual, or so we thought.

What they don't tell you in the guidebooks is Florida law apparently dictates there be a homemade food stand every thirty feet or so on every desolate country road. I'm not sure how they stay alive out there, but I have to admire the strange cross between Ayn Rand's capitalistic spirit and the homespun soul of Hee Haw. They sell anything that grows on trees or can be pulled from the ground: boiled peanuts, watermelons, oranges, tomatoes, strawberries, grapefruit, and a million other things you and I would assume only animals would eat. I even saw a place on Highway 27 where they sell goat milk fudge. I don't even want to know what that tastes like or how it's extracted.

Yeah, yeah. I'm getting to the point. I'm building atmosphere here.

Anyway, we're driving down the road and we see this stand outside Arcadia on highway 17. It's gone now, so don't bother looking for it. Trish says she wants some watermelon, so I pull the rental car into the parking lot and we get out. She walks over to the pallets of fruit and vegetables, and I start checking the tires. You can't be too careful on those roads down there with nails and rattlesnake fangs and God knows what else on those steaming roads waiting to pierce a tire or come flying up through the windshield into your skull.

I walk over to the far side, and I see this filthy kid wearing nothing but a diaper splashing around up to his waist in the muddy, oily water of a roadside ditch. He looks up at me, smiles, and then waves to me. Only his hand wasn't a hand—it looked like some fleshy gray flipper. It had no fingers, but it bent inward and wiggled at me. I almost threw up right then. Instead (with great restraint), I grimaced at him, got back in the car, started the engine, and revved it a few times to get Trish going. All the while, I'm staring straight ahead trying not to look into the ditch. It's calling to me with this happy, chattering voice I couldn't understand.

Trish is over there choosing from this bin of battered brown melons laughing it up with one of the toothless locals. I honk the horn, she pays for the food, and then gets back in the car.

I spin out of the lot in a spray of dust and zoom down the highway, looking at the rearview mirror to make sure that hideous thing isn't crawling on the trunk or something. Trish, clueless as ever, is going on and on about these melons she just bought, and how delicious they are, and how they only come from Arcadia. Meanwhile, all I'm doing is putting distance between the car and that degenerate little freak.

A few minutes later, I told Trish about the kid and his gnarled, stumpy flipper, and she got mad at me for being scared of him. "He's just handicapped, dear," she said. "Imagine all the people who run away from him and never care who he is."

The guilt of that sunk in for a few miles and I once again found myself grateful to have Trish in my life. She could always look at things in ways that never occurred to me. Still, those people in that town were scary and I had no intention to return there. Handicapped or not, these are not the people I want assembling my Quarter Pounder at the local McDonalds, if you know what I'm saying.

No, no. That's isn't the end. If I had just seen a kid with a flipper, everything would be fine. I'd have chalked it up to one of those "grandmother - nephew" relationships they have there below the Mason-Dixon line and left it at that. But there was more in store for us, I'm sorry to say.

We kept driving the rest of that day and the next. You've never seen such flat terrain in your life or so many primal-looking plants. I half-expected a dinosaur head to pop up from behind one of those clumps of palmetto bushes and screech some ancient cry in my direction. The only thing that convinced me I hadn't traveled back in time was all of the concrete block structures along the road. Bowling alleys, trailer park offices, convenience stores - everywhere we drove, sunbleached buildings baked in the heat.

All the while, Trish is eating these melons. She offered some to me, but it looked too mushy and greasy to eat. But Trish is the adventurous one (having sipped from a pool at Carlsbad Caverns and eaten wild berries on the road to Walden Pond), so she ate those things down to the rinds.

The next day (after a horrible night in a lousy insect-infested motel) we were still driving across this wasteland when we decided we'd had enough of central Florida and started heading for the coast. Trish and I talked and daydreamed about waterfront hotels and pleasant beaches, and we could hardly wait to get to a decent highway to cross over to the gulf.

We were driving up Highway 27 looking for a highway going west when Trish started having a stomachache. We'd just eaten at a Hardees restaurant, so I thought it was just indigestion. Then she got nauseous, but every time we stopped, she just couldn't get anything out. She'd just stand there hacking and hacking.

We kept driving, and she kept getting worse and worse, so I started looking for a hospital. Somewhere out here there had to be a hospital. Children are born there, right? People get sick, don't they? I drove for miles, but didn't see anything.

Trish starts convulsing in her seat, with frothy saliva gurgling past her lips. I'm frantic now, screaming down the highway at 90 miles an hour, honking the horn to get some other driver's attention, but there's nothing out there but acres of palmetto and abandoned gas stations. I'm afraid to stop because the next curve in the road could hide a hospital or a payphone.

Finally, I see on the horizon this orange hemisphere and a huge tacky sign that said Orange World or Citrus King or some other lousy name. Right then, my wife's stomach exploded, and her blood sprayed all over the inside of the car. We both scream, hers much shorter than mine and fading into a helpless choking noise. I'm rocking the wheel back and forth on the road, not sure what to do next, tears stinging my eyes.

My scream was soon overwhelmed by the tiny screeching of fifty gray, eel-like creatures writhing from her body cavity and devouring their way free through her flesh with their little jaws and tusks.

I panicked. I veered through the lanes of the road across the grass toward that goddamned orange dome hoping someone there could help us. Meanwhile, the eels are finishing her off, and I'm trying to whip them away with my hand, but they just keep nipping at me. I hit a mailbox and it rolls over the hood, windshield, roof, and trunk of the car with a series of clanks.

By the time I spun the car into the parking lot, she was gone except for loose fingers and bones sticking with streaks of gore on the upholstery. Beneath my seat, I could feel them slithering around, looking for a way to get to me. I slammed on the brakes just as one had begun to wrap around my ankle. Then I threw open the door and rolled from the car into the unpaved parking lot, kicking the thing off my leg and into the grass.

As I lay there in the sand, the sinister little creatures oozed through the open car door and splashed into the weeds of a drainage ditch. Then they were gone.

I looked up, and a whole crowd had gathered around gawking at me, not surprised at the things emerging from my car. One held a cypress clock with the poem "Footprints" etched into the wood. Another wore a tattered, bleached out Mickey Mouse shirt with the sleeves torn off. A third snapped pictures of the inside of my car.

And there, on the seat, were the pieces of what had once been the woman I loved. They wouldn't find her bloody wedding ring under the seat until later.

I don't know why I did what I did then. Maybe it was the whole surreal atmosphere, or the heat, or some existential joy of having survived.

I laughed - long, explosively, and maniacally. They had to lash me down to the stretcher to get me to the hospital, with me cracking jokes and grinning all the while. I laughed even longer when they told me the next day my wife had suffered from flesh-eating bacteria. "Those are the biggest goddamned bacteria I've ever seen!" I cried. "Those fuckers could pull a plow!"

What do you do after your wife is devoured alive by gray slithering worms? Believe it or not, there isn't a lot of support out there for a man widowed by the minions of evil. They don't have books about it in the self-help section at Barnes and Noble with titles like "I'm OK, You're Scary" or "Chicken Soup for the Damned Soul." You can't talk to your best buddy about it at the local bar, you can't ask your psychologist what to do, and God forbid you even mention it to your pastor.

I tried going to a church group for widowed men, but it just didn't work out. It was hard to keep a straight face when those poor old geezers asked how my wife died. They kept pressing me and pressing me about it until I finally told them she cried out "This sow is mine!" at the drive-up window at the White Castle and the town elders voted to burn her at the stake.

I walked away from there laughing so hard I almost wet myself.

My psychiatrist called it "a need to sublimate my anger with humor." My boss called it "a sad call for help from a seriously demented and morbid man" right before he fired me for giggling over the pictures of maimed clients in court.

With my new spare time, I found myself reading a lot of horror novels and true crime books, mostly for laughs. You'd be surprised how funny a book like "Rosemary's Baby" can be if you have the right attitude.

Then, in a spasm of guilt, I tried to kill myself but failed miserably.

As I lay there on the bed with the shotgun still smoking and the blast pattern of bird shot splattered across my bedroom wall a good five feet away from any part of my head, I realized something: the laughter I couldn't stop was the only thing that could save me. It was the only way I could let out the pain, like bursts of steam from a locomotive.

In a flash of inspiration, I remembered something about all of those horror books and stories: there are four ways to confront total evil. One is to go mad (which was out of the question). Another is to run away (which one cannot do from absolute evil). Another is to fight, however vainly, to survive (which was hopeless). I chose a fourth possibility: to laugh. And that is what saved me.

When I discovered there are things lurking in those ditches in Florida waiting for the right moment to feast themselves on our bodies, I knew everything I had assumed about the universe was wrong. There's more out there than we can imagine, and it doesn't fit nicely into our existing views of the world. I can't fight it, so I do the only thing that's left to me: I mock it. I reduce the horror to something small and manageable by laughing at it. And I make others laugh at it, too.

How do you fight the Devil and his children? How do you resist the onslaught of slithering creatures from Beyond? I have no idea. The best thing I can think of, though, is to laugh at them. Every time we make fun of evil, it shrinks a little more. Maybe we can get it small enough to stomp it dead. Who knows?

With that, he pointed the bottom of his glass into the air and swallowed the remaining liquor with a single gulp. He slammed the glass on the bar.

"Stick around for another set, buddy. It's a little blue." He winked at me and walked backstage.

I decided not to stay.

Grandpa, What Happens When We Die?

First, shrieking demons
breathe icy needles down your body,
licking their black lips like starving orphans at
Thanksgiving.

Then, mad laughter
bubbles from the antechambers of Hell,
carrying you through fetid air
down the dark, craggy tunnels of Satan's colon.

Your friends, your family, your loves all damned
moan in sadness as you plunge
like an anchor from the garbage-strewn barge of pain.

Your cruelest words slice your ears.
Your basest act crushes your hands to splinters.
Your cowardice twists your feet into tentacles.

> Your eyes boil.
> Your nose melts.
> Your teeth crumble like Stonehenge.

The next day gets worse.

So today:
> Run. Play. Laugh. Love. Shout.
> For tomorrow might not be as good.

Story Notes

Anomie

This is a true story.

Well, the first half, anyway. My friend William labors at the convenience store depicted in this tale and has done so for fifteen years; he claims he's using his psychology degree for a longitudinal study of the underclass in Tampa. When I once complained about the spiritual hollowness of a cubicle job, he scoffed and revealed the true horrors of being one bad customer away from being shot or knifed for a carton of cigarettes.

I just embellished from there.

"Anomie" first appeared in issue 11 of *Dark Muse.*

And Justice for Doll

I don't understand mysteries. That is, how do you maintain such a huge market of mystery novels when—let's face it—there's a finite number of crimes to commit, a finite number of ways of committing them, and a finite number of reasons to do so? Setting aside the random sickos, any police detective can tell you that the person who had a stake in performing the crime did it: the ex-boyfriend, the ex-wife, the money-hungry children.

Criminals aren't that creative, and I'm sure mystery writers have far surpassed them. Still, they try. Sometimes it's with strange detectives: "He's a gay Republican car salesman, but he also solves crimes!" Other times, it's with historical mysteries: "Halt, Spartan dog! Thou carriest a knife by cover of darkness!"

We're running out of good mystery stories, and I had to get one last one in before Law and Order took them all.

"And Justice for Doll" first appeared in the September 2003 issue of *Alfred Hitchcock's Mystery Magazine.*

Nessmas

Remember that old television show "In Search Of"? You know, the one with Leonard Nimoy narrating baldly credulous stories about mysterious phenomena with just the right mid-seventies mix of New Age lunacy and pseudo-scientific babble? They did episodes on almost every crackpot idea to ever occur to the human race, and—being a kid when I watched them—I fell for them all.

Nessie was particularly compelling, and (even this late in my cynical development) still seems among the more plausible strange things in our world. Though my belief in UFOs, ghosts, ESP, and all of the other things I read about when I was ten has waned, I still accept the possibility of ancient lifeforms eking out their lives in the far reaches of the planet. The coelacanth and giant squid represent two real-life examples, and maybe Nessie is one of those, too.

The coelacanth and the giant squid, however, have one characteristic that sets them apart from Nessie, but I wrote this story to bridge that gap.

A note to Scottish readers: I don't have a damned clue about Scotland or what goes on there. Me speculating about the sights and sounds of Loch Ness is like Ray Bradbury speculating about the surface of Mars in the early fifties.

"Nessmas" first appeared as "Nessmass" in issue 11 of *Whispers from the Shattered Forum*.

Speaking Mouth Dog

I'm surprised that literary theorists don't have a greater reputation for horror. After all, what can be more existentially disturbing than the idea that, say, we are merely the mouthpieces of random and meaningless language, or that the greatest literary soaring of our spirits are just signs of a our culturally-ingrained socioeconomic position?

Indeed, I wrote this story in nearly a single sitting while reading before one of my Master's classes. The essay was one by Kristeva, and about two paragraphs into it, I wondered aloud, "Is this a put on?"

Then, in a flash of inspiration that almost every post-modernist literary critic would consider to be a function of class, history, psychology, or diet, the idea struck me for a story about the perfect critical theory test subject.

Meet Broman Sumner, the man your professors fear.

"Speaking Mouth Dog" is original to this collection. It won first place in the University of North Florida graduate fiction competition.

The Trespasser

I have continued to maintain that our twisted universe has mistakenly (or, worse, with cruel deliberation) taken a person with the sensibilities and priorities of a 19th century aristocrat and thrust him into this century to write horror stories without the benefit of a crumbling mansion or dwindling family fortune.

My inborn disdain for the common man, my deep resistance to all forms of labor: these are sure signs I belong in a gentler age—or at least in the top echelon of a more brutal one. I should be penning monographs in the parlor of my estate and taking long bicycle rides to make etchings of ancient family tombstones, not suffering the indignities of Wal-Mart.

This story reveals my true nature and priorities. Before finding its true home in Cemetery Dance, several editors criticized the story by saying, "Try to write in your natural voice." Well, uh, that is my natural voice.

Snooty critics, rejoice: I wrote this story during lectures in a Psychological Approaches to Literature class, and—though I didn't consciously do so—I'm sure you can find dozens of interesting parallels and connections. If it helps, the psychological theories we used were Abraham Maslowe's and Karen Horney's. Have fun!

"The Trespasser" first appeared in issue 40 of *Cemetery Dance.*

Billy

Political conviction is trendy these days, isn't it? We paste bumper stickers on our cars, hoist flags in front of our houses, and pontificate over complex foreign policy issues over our bad novelty drinks at the Chili's bar. There's a wonderful endorphin rush from taking a stand—even if we don't believe it. To be right even for a fraction of a second is worth the sad realization down the road that we were horribly misled.

My former boss is probably the only consistent animal rights advocate I'd ever met. She doesn't just send checks to PETA or restrict her diet to chicken or fish: she saves injured animals, volunteers at the local animal shelter, and avoids every item that ever had anything to do with an animal. She eats absolutely no meat, wears no leather, drinks no milk, uses no butter.

I admire the consistency of her conviction. True, I eat enough meat to offset her efforts, but I'm still impressed she resists all of society's pressure. Keep up the good work!

"Billy" first appeared at *Horrorfind.com*.

Cthulhu Fhtagn, Baby!

This story has the virtue of being my first accepted tale. I almost threw away the contracts when I got them.

The then-publisher of Weird Tales, Warren Lapine, had developed a marketing juggernaut to increase the circulation and prestige of his publishing empire, partly through direct mailings to subscribers. If you enjoy *Dreams of Decadence*, why not try *Weird Tales* or *Fantastic Stories of the Imagination*?

I'd just mailed in my Weird Tales renewal when I received an envelope from DNA Publications. "For the love of God," said I. "Are they dunning me for another subscription already?" Leaning over the trashcan, though, I realized the envelope was heavier than the standard subscription flyer, and when I tore it open, a contract fell out.

It's a good thing, too; I'd hate for the public to be deprived of the obligatory Lovecraft pastiche of my career. Every horror writer is required to write one, but—thankfully—not required to publish it.

"Cthulhu Fhtagn, Baby!" first appeared in issue 327 (spring 2002) of *Weird Tales*.

Soured

Every child endures a horrible experience at least once in his or her life. After an idyllic couple of years thinking that Mommy simply manufactures dinner in a surgically-sterile pantry while wearing a biohazard suit, someone finally breaks the news: yes, sometimes a clump of greasy hair slithers out from under the lunch lady's cap and into your peach cobbler. Yes, sometimes there's a yellowed tooth floating in the Spaghetti-Os.

It's the end of culinary innocence, and no one is ever the same again. I certainly wasn't.

This story is about a similar revelation.

A disclaimer: I do love milk so very, very much, even after writing this story. I'd drink it no matter what, even if…

"Soured" first appeared at *Horrorfind.com*. It received an Honorable Mention in the *Year's Best Fantasy and Horror 18th Annual Collection*.

Portrait of the Horror Artist as a Young Man

My father for all his faults has a sort of evil nobility: between stretches of questionable behavior and ethics, he does something heroic or principled.

It will probably make you feel better to believe that the story that follows came only from my twisted imagination, though the truth is that it also came from his.

"Portrait of the Horror Artist as a Young Man" first appeared in the anthology *Small Bites*.

Raw Recruits

My parents believe in spirits and consider it their mission to convert me to a less concrete mode of thinking.

One of the proofs they offered after my grandmother died was to show me a picture of her drawn by a magic box. The medium holds the box, channels the spirit, and colored pencils scratch around inside to make the drawing.

When I saw the picture, I noticed there was no hair and it was very small. In short, it could have been any elderly person. That explanation didn't convince them, though, so I brought out the big guns.

"Could Grandmother draw when she was alive? How did she learn that in heaven?"

That's my issue with communicating with the dead. Suddenly, they're different. Nobody summons the spirit of an angry drunken grandfather that says, "Hey, shithead. You disappointed me when I was alive and you still suck." It's all kindness and spirit. They're smarter, friendlier, and more generous than they were when they were alive. And of course, they never lie.

"Raw Recruits" first appeared in the Fall 2004 issue of *Outer Darkness*.

Representative Sample

The universe has a balancing system of its own, and we need only be patient. The girl who dumped you at the prom will one day appear on television as all 600 pounds of her is lifted via helicopter from her bathroom.

The problem, though, is that I don't have the patience to let the universe mete its justice. I'm annoyed the universe isn't willing to use me more often as a tool of that justice. I'm creative. I'm funny. It seems a waste not to put me to good use.

I love a good revenge story. It's a very American form, really: the story of our nation is almost a revenge tale. Settled by the castoffs of every nation, we roll up our sleeves to prove to people who wronged us that we're better than they are. Sure, the Founding Fathers had some positive motivations, but I'm sure they weren't unhappy to stick it to their British oppressors.

There are few underdogs like space exploration. Artemis magazine is the fiction arm of an organization called the Moon Society working to get humans back on our planet's satellite to exploit some resources and develop new technologies. I met Ian Randall Strock (the editor) at Balticon in 2001 and decided to write about the eventual triumph of their aims—by hook or by crook.

"Representative Sample" first appeared in issue 7 (summer 2002) of *Artemis*.

Bingo

I like the idea of working animals. When I see those seeing eye dogs with their signs, "Do not pet me. I am a seeing eye dog," I'm always tempted to pet them anyway. I mean, the owner can't see me doing it, right?

Police dogs, of course, are wonderful. I'm glad they've invented Kevlar vests for them and that they're taken care of after they retire.

I just worry about how such a dog eases into his retirement.

"Bingo" first appeared in the April 2004 issue of *Alfred Hitchcock's Mystery Magazine*.

You're Welcome

See, I'm really supposed to be writing love stories.

I'm a romantic, fond of pronouncements of endless love and affection, enamored with the endorphin rush of early attraction. We need more passion in our lives, and the rush of chemicals we get from the pressing of lips may be the only way some of us can get the feeling of real purpose and direction: make new samples of our DNA.

Of course, I am also a twisted, demented person better kept outside in a wooden shanty than allowed into the parlor, and my fiction reflects this.

So this is my best shot at a love story. You can try reading it to your lover while feeding each other strawberries on a picnic blanket, but I suspect it might get results you don't expect.

"You're Welcome" is original to this collection.

Solidity

Bums fascinate me. Not in any trendy liberal "let's help them" kind of way—mostly just a morbid curiosity. I've thought of getting a degree in psychology, but I don't have the heart to tell some department counselor that I'd just be doing it to know more about how things can go horribly and fascinatingly wrong with the human noggin.

Bums, of course, are somehow messed up in the head, right? They're living in the most financially successful civilization in the history of the world and are surrounded by literally thousands of opportunities to make money either honestly or dishonestly, and they choose their own unknowable agenda instead. They squat beneath Calvin Kline billboards and push shopping carts past movie marquees, and they don't give a damn about any of it. They're immune to societal pressure.

When I worked in Washington D.C., I encountered many of the bums described in this story. They don't mention it in the brochures, but Washington is a prime laboratory for an amateur vagrant sociologist like myself; they seem to be attracted there by...well, by the irony, if nothing else. Even a guy wearing one worn mitten knows there's something obtuse about sleeping in newspapers at the feet of the Lincoln Memorial.

"Solidity" first appeared in the anthology *Travel Guide to the Haunted Mid-Atlantic.*

Exit Laughing

To characterize my feelings about Florida as "mixed" would be something of an understatement. Although I enjoyed the open spaces and convenience of a slightly-populated area, I must confess that I wasn't not as fond of the searing heat, pony-sized insects, or doddering elderly weaving between lanes of traffic.

For all its virtues and flaws, however, Florida has been only lightly plumbed for its horrific potential. We've read about crumbling stone houses in Massachusetts or decadent vine-circled mansions in New Orleans, but no one has written much about sun-bleached beach shanties or festering swamps.

To the great chagrin of the state chamber of commerce, I'm doing everything I can to shatter those positive stereotypes.

"Exit Laughing" first appeared in issue 6 of *Delirium* and later at *Horrorfind.com.*

Grandpa, What Happens?

My beef with many of the religions of the world is that they don't instill proper reverence for the world in which we currently live. It's all about the afterlife. The principles of many of the world's religions can be summed up as, "Just wait until your father comes home." You're either going to get a spanking (Hell) or candy (Heaven).

I hope I'll one day be a crazy enough coot to tell a child something like this.

"Grandpa, What Happens When We Die?" is original to this collection.

Acknowledgements

No man is an island, blah blah blah. The following people share at least some of the blame for this book so save some of your ire and ammunition for them.

Steve Berman, my erstwhile friend and Lethe Press CEO, in addition to making this book a reality, also offers good advice and friendship.

Matt Warner, my blunt and surly comrade-at-arms in the battle against genre mediocrity, helps goad me on to better stories. In return, I goad him on to embarrassing arguments with genre personalities.

Deena Warner, my cover artist, has the uncanny knack of understanding the aesthetics of Willness—a troubling gift, to be sure.

Darrell Schweitzer, Ian Randall Strock, Brian Keene, Linda Landrigan, Cullen Bunn, and Richard Chizmar gave me my first acceptances. Without them, I'd have simply retired to a cabin in the woods to write manifestoes.

Don Rochester, Tom Phillips, Richard Soehner, and Ray Rodil read and heard early drafts of the work you see here, and yet they (and I) survived to offer them to the public. So, too, have Jason Carraway, Scott McClellan, Paul Faile, Ed Ralph, Chris Harben, Mac McDonald, and Raymond Champion offered their attention, feedback, and friendship.

Janet Carter and Matt Holloman provided early encouragement in the terrible town documented in the story, "Exit Laughing." They kept me from eating the melons, and for that, I'm thankful.

William Simmons is one of those brave souls who continue to show me just how important it is to be brave and steadfast about the things you love or else risk losing your soul.

My family (Dianne and Larry Hall, Karen and Martin Simpson, Andrew Hall, Katie and Emily Simpson) offered the perfect mixture of humor and horror in which to grow up.

Aimee Payne is, well, my favorite.

About Will Ludwigsen

Born in a log cabin in the Ozark mountains to a simple but hard-working farm family, Will grew up learning the home-spun wisdom of his elders as well as developing an almost Mozart-like talent for playing the gut bucket.

That's not strictly true. Indeed, very little that Will says ever is.

Born confused between the difference between fantasy and reality, between books and life, Will hasn't bothered to reconcile the two. He recently completed both a Master of Arts in English from the University of North Florida as well as the Clarion workshop for genre fiction. With these tools, he writes horror non-fiction for the Federal government and horror fiction for you.

His short stories have appeared in magazines such as *Alfred Hitchcock's Mystery Magazine, Cemetery Dance,* and *Weird Tales*. He has a small but dedicated fan following among society's dregs and dropouts, people too sociopathic to qualify for the Manson family. They gather at http://www.will-ludwigsen.com for all of the latest news about Will's crimes.

Above all else, however, Will writes: compulsively, intractably, like a train bearing down on a damsel lashed to the tracks in a 1920s silent movie.

You're the damsel. Enjoy!

Printed in the United Kingdom
by Lightning Source UK Ltd.
134554UK00001B/245/A